Her cheeks were pink, her striking eyes downcast as she disconcerted him by reaching for the pen and scrawling her signature on the document that Dario had given him.

"You shouldn't sign a legal document without your own lawyer at hand to represent your interests," Gaetano remarked tautly.

"That's your world, not mine," Lara parried in a tone of scorn. "I don't require a lawyer to tell me I want to be free of you. You have disappointed me in every conceivable way, Gaetano—"

"I regret that you feel that way," he breathed curtly. "That was not my goal."

"No, your only goal is that I sign this form so that you can shed any responsibility you might have for me as discreetly as possible. That doesn't surprise me, but I'm angry on my son's behalf!" Lara countered, throwing her head back. "He is an innocent party here and you didn't even look at him at the park!"

"You're trying to say that your son is also...my son?" Gaetano framed in open disbelief.

"He's sixteen months old, Gaetano. Who else could be his father?"

The Stefanos Legacy

The billionaire's vow to reunite his family!

When his father dies, renowned Greek tycoon Aristaeus Stefanos is devastated. Not only at the loss of his beloved father, but also the shocking discovery that his father had feet of clay—in the form of two secret daughters!

Ari will do anything to track down his half sisters and offer them his protection—his sense of honor demands nothing less. But his priorities are turned upside down when it's revealed he also has an orphaned baby niece. Ari must put his quest to find his long-lost family on hold to focus on the tiny infant who needs him—and on finding the bride he needs to claim his niece!

Read Ari and Cleo's story in
Promoted to the Greek's Wife

Read Giovanni and Leah's story in
The Heirs His Housekeeper Carried

Read Gaetano and Lara's story in
The King's Christmas Heir

Read the extraordinary trilogy from
USA TODAY bestselling author Lynne Graham

Available now!

Lynne Graham

—

THE KING'S CHRISTMAS HEIR

PRESENTS™

ISBN-13: 978-1-335-58378-9

The King's Christmas Heir

Copyright © 2022 by Lynne Graham

Harlequin Enterprises ULC
22 Adelaide St. West, 41st Floor
Toronto, Ontario M5H 4E3, Canada
www.Harlequin.com

Printed in U.S.A.

Lynne Graham was born in Northern Ireland and has been a keen romance reader since her teens. She is very happily married to an understanding husband who has learned to cook since she started to write! Her five children keep her on her toes. She has a very large dog who knocks everything over, a very small terrier who barks a lot and two cats. When time allows, Lynne is a keen gardener.

Books by Lynne Graham

Harlequin Presents

The Greek's Convenient Cinderella
The Ring the Spaniard Gave Her

Heirs for Royal Brothers

Cinderella's Desert Baby Bombshell
Her Best Kept Royal Secret

Innocent Christmas Brides

A Baby on the Greek's Doorstep
Christmas Babies for the Italian

The Stefanos Legacy

Promoted to the Greek's Wife
The Heirs His Housekeeper Carried

Visit the Author Profile page
at Harlequin.com for more titles.

For my daughter, Rachel, and her unswerving support.

PROLOGUE

THE SNOW WAS falling in a blinding blur that ensured that the hiker couldn't see more than a foot ahead of him. He was colder than he had ever known it was possible to be, which didn't say much for his top-flight protective gear or the countless ski trips he had enjoyed since childhood. Those experiences had convinced him that he was a tough mountain man capable of handling anything that the weather could throw at him.

Too late now to realise how imprudent he had been, he acknowledged grimly. Vittorio's illness had knocked him for six and his brother's demand that he go off and live his own life while he suffered had almost sent him off the rails. He was neither impulsive nor foolish, but he had *needed* solitude to accept both Vittorio's diagnosis and his wishes. In the grip of terrible grief, he had scorned the trappings of his world: the bodyguards, the five-star accommodation and private jets. That lifestyle attracted attention like a flashing neon light, and he didn't want that. It had not once occurred to him that going fashionably off grid could endanger him. Innately confident, he had seen himself as mature and invincible. He had even argued about making a monthly phone call home, ostentatiously ditching his phone before his departure. He was twenty-seven years old…how mature had either of those decisions been?

Now that he was lost and likely to die of exposure such trivial concerns seemed a million miles from his current daunting reality. His confused, self-critical thoughts were drifting, blurring, his steps no longer sure in the heavy snow. Hypothermia, he guessed abstractedly, hitching his rucksack, which seemed to grow heavier with every second. In an abrupt movement, he began to struggle free of its weight and as he stepped forward again, feeling much lighter and freer, he caught a glimpse of lights and stared in disbelief through the falling snow at the small outdoor tree illuminated with a colourful string of lights. There was a house with a garden at the foot of the hill. He didn't like Christmas. Indeed, he had never enjoyed Christmas, but that evidence of civilisation had never been a more welcome sight. As he descended the steep slope with the haste of impatience, he lost his footing and skidded into a fall that made him shout. He fell backwards, struck his head a glancing blow on a rock and knew no more…

CHAPTER ONE

Two years later

HIS MAJESTY, KING GAETANO of the European country of Mosvakia, paced by the window of his private office as he awaited the arrival of his best friend and legal advisor, Dario Rossi.

Dario had phoned him to tell him that the investigation agency had finally found *her*, and Gaetano was eager to hear the details. Not because he was particularly interested in what his estranged wife might be doing or where she was living, he assured himself, but simply out of natural human curiosity.

Although there was nothing particularly natural about the predicament he had got himself into just over two years earlier, he conceded sardonically, his lean, darkly handsome face tense with scornful recollection. While suffering from temporary amnesia,

Gaetano had managed to marry a woman he had known for barely six weeks, a woman whom he knew virtually nothing about. Gaetano, prior to that act of inexplicable insanity, had been a playboy prince, notorious for his affairs and dislike of stuffy conventions such as getting married and maintaining a royally respectable low profile. So, what the hell had come over him after that accident in the mountains?

Two years on, Gaetano was still struggling to answer that baffling question. And to underline the obvious mistake he had made in marrying the woman, his bride had *deserted* him at dizzying speed. Gaetano, the son of a mother who had abandoned him as a toddler, had little sympathy for lying, disloyal women who walked out on their responsibilities. That he should also have married the same sort of woman infuriated him and it only emphasised how unsuitable the wife he had chosen had been. Most particularly a woman who had told him she loved him only hours before running away from him when he had needed her the most.

Mosvakia was a small country on the Adriatic coast, which had been in meltdown for the first year of Gaetano's return home. Vittorio had had leukaemia but instead of the long slow decline he had envisaged, Gaetano's older brother had died very suddenly from a heart attack. There had been no time for the careful training and transfer of power that Vittorio had planned for his little brother, no time for final goodbyes either.

Even worse, there had been neither the space nor the privacy for Gaetano to grieve or freak out about the huge responsibility of the throne that had become his without warning. Gaetano had had to bury his personal feelings deep and keep it together for the sake of the Mosvakian people. Wild ideas like abdication had had to be firmly squashed when the streets had filled with candle-holding crowds mourning his brother's demise. Loyalty and respect for Vittorio's dutiful example had gripped him hard.

He had toiled through the endless weeks of official mourning, the solemn state funeral rites and his own subsequent coronation like an automaton, simply making the speeches and performing the duties that were expected of him in his new and unfamiliar role as monarch. Like the rest of Mosvakia, Gaetano had still been reeling in total shock because Vittorio had been the brightest jewel in the Mosvakian crown and an impossible act to follow.

Furthermore, nobody had *ever* expected Gaetano to follow his sibling and end up as King. He was the second son, born from their father's brief second marriage, the literal spare to match the heir. Twenty years older than Gaetano and already having ruled for almost as long, Vittorio had married at the age of forty. Everyone had assumed that an heir would arrive quickly after his marriage to Giulia, only sadly, that long-awaited event hadn't happened, and then poor Vittorio had fallen ill.

Only months into Gaetano's reign, senior courtiers had begun to hint that Gaetano should now consider finding a bride. He had thought about the runaway wife who nobody but Dario knew he had, and he had duly redoubled his efforts to trace her and get a divorce. She had been impossible to find, with no social media presence.

Suddenly, memory sliced in like a shot of lightning to throw his rational thought processes into chaos. He remembered a tiny woman with a mass of strawberry-blonde hair and huge aquamarine eyes that dominated her delicate freckled face, a woman standing in front of a Christmas tree covered with multi-coloured lights. She was smiling, always smiling at him as though he lit up her world. His first sight of her and then the images and the remembered jumble of thoughts became distinctly cringeworthy. Why? Unbelievably, Gaetano, the heartbreaker and sexually unfettered cynic, had developed a severe case of insta-lust or insta-love, whatever people called that overwhelmingly immediate desire to possess another human being body and soul.

Gaetano blinked and gritted his teeth hard, annoyance flashing through him that those disturbing, illogical memories could still infiltrate his brain when he relaxed his guard even for a moment. Even two years on, she had left a mark on him that, it seemed, nothing could fully eradicate, and it outraged his pride. He turned with relief when a knock sounded on the door and Dario strode in clutching a file and looking nothing short of triumphant.

'At last!' Dario proclaimed, slapping the file down on Gaetano's desk, a tall, rangy male with a neatly clipped beard and a ready smile, a close friend since childhood. 'Now we can sort out that little problem of yours and return your life to normal.'

Gaetano frowned at that choice of words. 'Regrettably, my life's never going to be normal again.' As soon as he voiced that absurd truth, he raised a lean brown hand in a gesture of immediate apology. 'Forget I said that. I know that I should be grateful that our people have accepted me so readily in Vittorio's place.'

'Don't apologise for admitting that you never wanted the throne. You weren't trained for it, and you don't enjoy the pomp and ceremony in the same way as Vittorio did. And don't look at me like that, I was *not* criticising your beloved brother,' the lawyer declared. 'I merely want to point out that Vittorio was by no means perfect.'

'He was a good king,' Gaetano cut in defensively.

'He was an introvert, and you are an extrovert. You excel at diplomacy, and you single-handedly rescued the crown estate from bankruptcy years ago. You are and were very different men with divergent strengths. Stop comparing yourself to him,' his old friend chided quietly. 'If it's any consolation, my wife thinks women prefer you because you're so handsome and I know that's a very silly comment on a serious situation, but it should at least make you laugh.'

'Carla often makes me laugh,' Gaetano responded with his flashing smile, even white teeth bright against his bronzed skin. He swallowed the urge to point out that he had been unable to enjoy his friends' company over cosy suppers in recent times because his new status made such casual outings almost impossible to arrange or enjoy.

Bodyguards and police now surrounded him wherever he went. His attempt to lessen that security presence and reduce the long list of rules he was supposed to follow for his own safety had been unwelcome. Having lost his grandfather to the sea, his father to a car accident and now a third king to ill health, the Mosvakian government currently viewed royals as extremely fragile beings in constant danger. And now that there was only *one* royal-born left? Everyone was scared that some random act of fate or violence could kill off Gaetano as well, especially when he had no heir to follow him.

As Gaetano leant back against the edge of his desk to study the file, silence fell. Dario ordered coffee while Gaetano rapidly scanned the initial listed facts, but he ended up staring at the single photograph on offer instead. It wasn't a very good photo, depicting as it did a young woman bundled up in a padded jacket against the wintry cold, a braid of reddish blonde hair escaping from the hood and only a slice of her pale freckled profile visible.

'She's…she's signed up for further education classes?' Gaetano breathed in surprise, his attention still locked to the photo.

'Yes, she mostly studies online. The two of you really didn't talk very much during those six weeks, did you?' the lawyer murmured. 'When you met Lara Drummond, she was working as a house-sitter.'

'She told me that she was a waitress and a cleaner!' Gaetano objected, his strong jaw-line clenching.

'That wasn't a lie. She's currently working evenings as a cleaner. I imagine she will be eager to agree to a quick divorce if you offer her a decent settlement,' Dario opined with cynical conviction.

'She's *not* a gold-digger!' Gaetano bit out defensively. 'If she'd wanted money, she would scarcely have run away from me and my jet-set life!'

'Gaetano… I'm your lawyer as well as being your friend. My primary goal is to protect you. You married her without a prenup and because of that she could ask for the shirt off your back and get it in a British court,' Dario warned him worriedly. 'But as things stand, *she* left *you.* You have lived apart for the requisite two years and a no-contest divorce is straightforward.'

Gaetano nodded in silence, struggling to get a grip on the emotions simmering up inside him, emotions he had successfully managed to suppress for most of his life. He was convinced that letting his emotions loose was what had plunged him into trouble in the first place. He hadn't known who he was when he first met Lara and his amnesia had made the most of that new exhilarating freedom to do and say as he liked. Without the restraints imposed by his birth and conditioning and the depressingly constant presence of the paparazzi, Gaetano had become a much more innocent, vulnerable version of his true self and he had allowed his emotional intensity to control him.

He was appalled by that truth and determined never ever to make such a mistake again. Vittorio had fallen in love several times with the wrong women before he finally married Giulia, a woman whom he'd loved only as a friend. Gaetano had grown up watching his brother get his heart broken, witnessing for himself how many gold-diggers and social climbers were willing to lie and cheat their way into Vittorio's life and pretend to be something they were not.

'Yes, a divorce should be straightforward. Of course, that is assuming that there is no chance that Lara Drummond's child could be yours?' Dario prompted, that question startling Gaetano out of his reflections.

'She has a *child*?' Gaetano exclaimed, incredulous at that news, stalking over to the window with the file and turning his back on his friend to read it again.

Lara had had a little boy but, as his birth certificate had yet to be tracked down, the investigation team could only make a rough guess at his age. *Eighteen* to *twenty-four* months? Gaetano counted dates inside his head, and he did it so painfully slowly that nobody would ever have guessed that he was gifted in the mathematical field.

'Evidently your runaway wife has not been living the celibate life in the same way that you have been,' his friend pronounced in a rueful undertone. 'It may well transpire that she was pregnant when you first met her. But no matter, it is, hopefully, another reason why she may well be happy to regain her freedom. The only evidence of a male in her life, however, is her landlord, who appears to be a friend.'

His strong jawline clenched like a rock, Gaetano swung back to face the other man. 'A *friend*?' he derided.

'The agency cannot be more precise because the landlord is a soldier deployed abroad and nobody has actually seen her with him.'

'But she's living in *his* house.'

'It was originally his parents' home and his sister lives there with her as well,' Dario slotted in wryly. 'So, no proof of anything untoward that could be useful to us.'

'You have my gratitude for keeping this businesslike,' Gaetano breathed, running a restive set of long brown fingers through his cropped black hair while resisting the temptation to smash a frustrated fist into the wall.

'You knew her for six weeks and you weren't exactly in your right mind during that time. I assume we can now proceed as planned?' Dario studied him expectantly.

Gaetano's dark as midnight gaze narrowed. 'No. I want to see her first…when I'm *in* my right mind. I want to know how I react to her now.'

'For many reasons that would be unwise,' his friend warned him, frowning. 'The press could catch on. You did nothing wrong in marrying her, but I know you would prefer that connection to stay out of the public domain. You could also meet her again and—'

'I'm not going to fall down the same rabbit hole a second time!' Gaetano scoffed with a contemptuous curl of his expressive mouth. 'I intend to see and speak to her without turning it into a confrontation. Have a little faith in me, Dario. I'm not a complete idiot. I know I need this divorce, but I also have to move past what happened with her and I don't think I can comfortably do that without seeing her one last time.'

Unaware that the life she had carefully rebuilt after getting her heart smashed to smithereens was about to crash into a major obstacle, Lara stepped out of the shower with a smile and began to dry her hair. She loved Saturday mornings because Alice gave the children breakfast, and she got a lie-in before taking the kids to the park. Sundays it was Lara's turn to rise early and look after their little monsters. She crammed her mass of strawberry-blonde hair into a clip at the base of her skull. It felt heavy and she frowned.

Maybe it was time to get her hair cut to a more manageable length. It was sentimental to think of her grandfather smoothing her braid and admiring how long her hair was getting. But it was downright suicidal to remember long brown fingers feathering through her hair on a pillow and telling her how silky and soft it was. A sharp little pain pierced her chest as self-loathing set up shop inside her again. Gaetano was impossible to forget. As far as experience went, she had gone from zero to sixty with Gaetano the instant she laid eyes on him. Messy black hair in need of a trim, strong jawline outlined in black stubble, eyes as dark as pitch, set deep below strong brows. So handsome he had made her pinch herself to check that she wasn't dreaming.

But in reality, she *had* been dreaming, Lara reminded herself doggedly, because only in a silly girlish dream would a guy like Gaetano have truly fallen in love with her. Little ordinary Lara, the world's most natural wallflower, the sort of girl whom most people overlooked and forgot. She lacked the hooks that attracted male attention. She was no good at flirting and her curves were of the modest variety. There was nothing exciting about her, nothing that made her stand out from the crowd and yet, for the space of a magical six weeks, Gaetano had made her feel like the most beautiful and desirable woman in the world.

And when he had emerged all at once from his loss of memory? Lara shivered and crammed those recollections back into the mental locked box where she kept all such damaging, hurtful things. Dwelling on the bad stuff didn't change anything or indeed ease the hurt of those experiences. And Gaetano had hurt her so badly that on one level she knew that she would never recover from their brief marriage. That was what happened when you thought you had found 'perfect' and then it all suddenly fell apart in your hands.

Gaetano had made her feel wanted and necessary to someone else for the first time in many years. He had valued her when others had not, he had *seen* her while others ignored her, not least her adoptive mother. His apparent love for her had seduced her into capitulating fast to his attraction, plunging them both headfirst into a whirlwind marriage. It was little wonder that she had run off once he'd emerged from his amnesia and regretted their relationship. Nor could she have borne telling him about their son because if he didn't want her or to be married, why would he want a child from his mistake?

Clad in worn jeans and a sloppy sweater to fend off the winter temperatures, Lara ate her toast standing while Alice's five-year-old daughter, Iris, fought with Lara's son, Freddy, over the bike. The bike belonged to Iris, but Freddy, who wasn't dexterous enough as yet to ride it, loved to sit on it and ring the bell. He pinned big dark expectant eyes on his mother, a guilt trip in a single glance. Freddy was a total drama llama, given to fiery tantrums and sobbing meltdowns. His intensity fascinated Lara, who had a quiet, calm nature, but it also reminded her painfully of his volatile, passionate father. Iris took the bike and Freddy flung himself down and sobbed noisily.

'If you want my advice,' her friend and one-time stepsister, Alice, whispered at her elbow, 'you won't take the bike with them to the park today.'

'He can't ride it anyway. He has to learn.' Lara knew that her son would only shout and scream louder if she tried to lift him off the floor. 'It's not fair to deprive Iris of her bike.'

'He is *so* stubborn,' Alice remarked in wonderment as Freddy kicked his feet and screamed while Iris wheeled her bike out to the small hall before walking back to try and comfort Freddy. She was a kind little girl, well aware of the fact that Freddy was still a baby. Freddy, however, was a pretty tall and sturdy toddler in spite of the reality that he was still only sixteen months old. He looked much older than he was because of his sheer physical size.

'He's a handful and no mistake.' Alice sighed, a tall, elegant brunette with blue eyes and long hair in a ponytail.

'Auntie Lara...?' Iris danced in the doorway, her energetic little body raring to go. 'Can we go now?'

Freddy stood up, tears magically dried as his mother helped him into his coat and buckled him into the pushchair. When Iris ran off to the swings at the park, Lara unclipped her son and lifted him onto the baby slide. He threw up his arms with pleasure as he whizzed down the slide. He stumbled clumsily off at the bottom to run back to her. He couldn't manage the steps on his own yet and it annoyed him when he saw other children climb alone, but then the other children were all older and steadier on their feet.

As Freddy ran over to watch Iris on the swing, Lara followed, thinking about the coffee she would treat herself to once the kids had had enough. Life was so busy that she truly valued her rare moments of relaxation. Alice worked from home as an accountant and the two women shared childcare, al-

though Lara was very aware that at present
Alice was doing more than her fair share because Freddy was not at school like Iris in the
mornings when Lara slept, and he required
more attention.

Lara was very fond of Alice and her
brother, Jack. Although Lara's mother had
divorced the twins' father after only eighteen months of marriage, Lara had stayed
in touch with her step-siblings. She was still
grateful that they hadn't blamed her for her
mother's change of heart and their father's
misery. Of course, they were well aware now
of how many different partners Eliza Drummond had loved and left, and of how Lara had
been forced to take refuge with her grandparents when she was sixteen because she had
begun to feel threatened by her mother's boyfriend. To say the least, Lara had had a colourful upbringing, although her early years
had started out quiet, secure and happy.

She had been adopted as a newborn baby
by Stewart and Eliza Drummond. Her father
had been a doctor and she had adored him.
Tragically he had died from an aneurysm
when she was nine and her adoptive mother
had subsequently made some very bad de-

cisions. Devastated by her husband's death, Eliza had flailed around like a boat without a rudder, her only goal seemingly to find a man to replace the one she had lost. Unfortunately, she had found more bad than good men. The bad ones had stolen her money and beaten her up and the good ones had bored her. Alice and Jack's father had been one of those rare, good men.

It was a long time since Lara had seen her mother. At sixteen she had moved in with her grandparents, her late father's mum and dad, and while living with them she had begun catching up on her education. As far as she knew her mother, who ran a bar in Spain, had not returned to the UK in recent years. Eliza didn't stay in touch with her adopted daughter. Lara's return to the UK seemed to have killed any further interest the older woman might have had in her. The hurt caused by that lack of interest was a familiar theme in Lara's life.

'Of course, you're adopted…it's not the same,' her father's sister, her aunt Jo, had once declared with a fatalistic shake of her head. 'You're not really related to the rest of us at all and we can't help remembering that because you don't look remotely like any of us. It's a shame my brother died, because he really did think of you as *his* daughter. I'm sorry you lost that relationship.'

Lara had often been desperately sorry on that score as well but there was no point crying over spilt milk. Now that she was also a parent, she had tried to leave her childhood disappointments behind her and move on.

As she took the children to feed the ducks, she noticed a man walking down the path on the far side of the lake. He was unusually well dressed for the park, clad in a dark formal overcoat worn over what looked like a suit underneath. He walked very upright with the easy confident glide of a predator and Lara froze, momentarily tense because even from this distance the man reminded her just a little of Gaetano, who had likewise possessed that almost feral grace of movement. This guy was also very tall and well built, with black hair and a bronzed complexion that spoke of warmer climes, but he wasn't close enough for her to get a better look at him.

Of course, it couldn't be Gaetano, she scolded herself irritably. What would the King of Mosvakia be doing in a small run-down urban park? Even less would he want to run the risk of being associated with her, the very ordinary woman he had mistakenly married! She had been a *huge* mistake on Gaetano's terms, Lara made herself recall. The colour that the breeze had stung into her cheeks disappeared as she remembered the last day she had seen him two years earlier.

'I married you… I actually *married* you?' Gaetano had realised in absolute horror, looking at her as though she must somehow have tricked him into becoming her husband, his recoil from the concept of being married to her etched in his shaken features as he studied her. 'What the hell have I done?'

'We'll deal with that problem later,' his friend and sidekick, Dario, had interrupted with smooth impatience. 'Right now, it's not important. What *is* important is that you come home to Mosvakia to recover from your ordeal. We've been worried sick about you for weeks!'

Lara remembered how it had felt to be lumped in as part of Gaetano's 'ordeal', her tummy clenching on a nauseous wave. She gathered up the kids and walked over to the coffee van. Of course she hadn't informed

Gaetano about the fact that he had a son. That would have been very bad news on his terms when he didn't even want Lara as a wife. And why would he?

There had been a time when she had stalked Gaetano on the Internet, hungrily absorbing every photo and atom of information, but the drip-drip effect of reading about his many, many affairs had soon cured her of that weakness. She had soon learned that the man she had married had a raunchy background with the models, actresses and socialites who had shared his bed. Seemingly, Gaetano had had no serious relationships in his past. He had pursued sex, rather than love, and none of his affairs had lasted long. In short, he was not the man she had fallen madly in love with, not the man she had happily married. He was, in truth, the 'Playboy Prince' he had been dubbed by the press.

Collecting her coffee, Lara sat down on one of the battered old chairs beside the van and watched Iris and Freddy chase a ball. Freddy fell over a couple of times and Iris dragged him up. She was a terrific big sister. Lara had often wished that she had had a sibling. Occasionally she had thought about the fact that she was adopted and that she might have blood relatives somewhere in the world, if only she had the guts to look into her back story. Unfortunately, the many hurts and letdowns meted out by her adoptive family had made her reluctant to risk inviting more disillusionment and disappointment into her life.

Across the grass lay the wooded area of the park and as she sipped her coffee she saw men emerge from below the trees and wondered what they were doing. They had a serious, professional look about them and she thought they might be police. Were they searching for someone? Their presence spooked her, and she glanced at the kids, ready to take them home even though she hadn't yet finished her coffee. Somehow, her usual relaxation in the winter sunshine was absent.

'Lara...?'

It was a voice Lara had believed she would never hear again, dark and deep, overwhelmingly male. But then almost everything about Gaetano was overwhelmingly male, she conceded as she sat there hunched, virtually afraid to lift her head because she was convinced that she was suffering some kind of auditory hallucination. Thoughts about

Gaetano had overloaded her self-discipline and raised her anxiety level, she told herself irritably.

On that thought she looked up and was totally stunned when Gaetano settled down into the rusty weathered chair opposite her, his brilliant dark eyes locked to her, black lashes a thick canopy over his piercing gaze. It was those eyes of his that got to her every time. Dark, hypnotically compelling and potent. Beneath his weight, the rickety chair squeaked in protest. He was six feet four inches tall with the wide shoulders and lean hips of an athlete. He was still breathtakingly beautiful. Her mouth ran dry, her lungs compressed, butterflies fluttered. An unwelcome tightening in her pelvis made her stiffen even more as her breasts pushed against the lace of her bra in concert.

Lara's hair was loose and tumbled round her shoulders, the strawberry blonde waves tossed by the breeze and framing her delicate face. She was not a beauty, Gaetano told himself, yet when he looked at her, he still couldn't take his eyes off her. Either she was impossibly pretty in her delicacy or simply incredibly sexy. And covered from head to toe in jeans and an unflattering padded coat, how the hell could she be sexy? Everything about Lara was natural and unstudied, from the freckles scattered across her nose to the sensible clothing she wore. She was quite unlike any woman he had ever met before and that was probably what had drawn him in.

And yet she *was* sexy, Gaetano acknowledged grudgingly, his attention lingering involuntarily on the full pink pout of her lips and the brilliant blue of her eyes. As his trousers stretched taut at the groin with an arousal he could barely credit, he tensed, flashes of memory returning to haunt him as they so often did in the dark of the night in his empty bed. Skinny but curvaceous, he recalled, so skinny he had tried to feed her up until she had confessed that she never ever put on weight. She was wild and impossibly sweet in bed, so receptive to his every move he hadn't been able to keep his greedy hands off her.

'You have five minutes with her before there's a risk of press intrusion,' his chief security officer had warned him.

He was already three minutes into that time limit, and he had been silent. 'We need to talk,' he informed her then with chilling gravity.

Lara felt that chill, that distance in Gaetano straight down to the marrow of her bones. She remembered his warmth, his intensity, and suddenly, that clear change in him shook her. She didn't know what she had expected from him. When she had first run away from him, she had had no plan. That had been a knee-jerk response to his wounding rejection. She had had no thought of what the future might bring and no suspicion that she was pregnant.

'Yes, we need to talk,' Lara conceded reluctantly, her gaze entrapped by glittering dark eyes enhanced by the lush fringe of ebony lashes. Mesmeric eyes teeming with raw allure. She swallowed the lump in her tight throat.

Gaetano slid a printed card across the small table. 'I'm staying at this address. I'll be waiting there for you this evening. If you want, I can send a car to pick you up.'

'That won't be necessary,' she whispered, grasping the card with nerveless fingers, dragging it down off the table into her pocket. For the sake of her pride, she had to take control of the encounter and intelligence had already suggested the most likely reason why Gaetano would seek her out after so long. And if that was true, that had to mean that their marriage had been legal, after all, she reasoned numbly. On the basis of that startling enough assumption, she said tightly, 'You want to discuss a divorce, don't you?'

Gaetano dealt her a cold hard appraisal, backed by the cold hard power of his forceful personality. 'What do you think?'

CHAPTER TWO

GAETANO STRODE AWAY and only then did Lara
draw breath again, sucking in the icy air like
a drowning swimmer. His appearance had
plunged her fathoms deep in shock. In the immediate aftermath she was annoyed that she
had not been the first to acknowledge their di-
lemma and take charge. *She* should have con-
tacted *him* to request a divorce, she reasoned
fiercely. But that would have meant throwing
Freddy into the mix and Freddy was another
question altogether. She didn't want to talk
about her son, but she couldn't lie about his
existence either.

Strapping Freddy into his pushchair, she
left the park with Iris to walk home. She
would have to meet Gaetano and put their
little winter idyll behind her where it belonged. And why was she so tense and worried? Gaetano had made a mistake marrying

her. The instant he had recovered his memory he had immediately recognised their marriage as a mistake. Why would he be any more interested in Freddy than he was in Freddy's mother?

'Are you going out tonight?' she asked Alice when she got back to the house, because Lara didn't clean at weekends and her friend usually went out with her boyfriend.

'No. It's a hot bath and an early night for me,' Alice announced with a roll of her expressive eyes.

'You're not seeing Jamie?'

'No, he took offence when I said it was too soon for me to meet his family, so we're on a break,' her friend divulged.

'You've been seeing him for months now,' Lara remarked carefully.

'I've done the "getting serious" thing once and I'm not interested in doing it again,' her friend told her squarely.

Lara bit her tongue because she knew her friend would get annoyed if she tried to persuade her otherwise. Alice had been engaged and Iris had been a toddler when her fiancé had died in a motorbike crash. Devastated by that loss, Alice had sworn off risking her heart again.

'Well, it suits me if you're staying in because I've got to go out tonight. Freddy's father came to speak to me in the park,' Lara confided.

Alice stared at her in surprise. 'Where did he come from? I thought he wasn't local.'

'He's not but obviously he's tracked me down and he wants a divorce. I've agreed to meet up with him this evening.'

'What about Freddy?'

Lara winced. 'We'll see.'

'You should've told the guy about his son ages ago.' Alice sighed. 'Some financial support would have made your life a lot easier.'

'It can't be a coincidence that he appeared in the park I visit every weekend,' Lara fielded ruefully. 'To find me he probably had to use a detective agency, so I'm pretty sure he would've found out about Freddy at the same time. And? He didn't even *look* in Freddy's direction…not once!'

'I wish you'd tell me more than the bare bones of what happened between you.'

'He got his memory back, Alice, and he didn't want me or what I thought we had any more,' Lara pronounced curtly. 'That's all you need to know.'

It wasn't that she didn't trust Alice, only that the finer details of her involvement with Gaetano and his precise status were just a little too sensational to share. Alice would not deliberately reveal Lara's secrets to anyone, but nobody liked to gossip more than Alice once she had had a couple of drinks. It had been less risky simply to leave her best friend partially in the dark and stick to sharing only the necessary facts.

The unembellished facts, Lara reminded herself, recollection tugging her back more than two years in time.

Two years ago she had been working as a waitress in a York café and living in the bedsit above until her boss had decided to retire and sell the building. In dismay at losing both employment and home together, Lara had discussed possible future plans with her closest friend at the time, Cathy, the older woman who'd managed the craft shop next door.

Realising that Lara was at a loose end, Cathy had then asked her if she would look after her house and her pets for several weeks over Christmas while she and her husband flew out to Australia to visit their daughter and their grandchildren. Having looked after Cathy's pets before at her remote farmhouse, Lara had been pleased to accept the invitation. It would give her a comfortable breathing space in which to decide what she wanted to do next with her life and allow her to enjoy Christmas in peace and tranquillity.

The day Gaetano arrived it was snowing heavily. Lara had spent a lazy day watching festive movies with the dogs and the cats. There were no close neighbours and no passing traffic because the single-track road to the farmhouse ended at its gates. In snow the steep road was virtually impassable, and she was relieved that she had shopped for fresh food only the day before.

Behind the house, a hilly outcrop of rock ran down to the edge of the garden. She was cleaning the kitchen when she heard the shout, and the dogs began barking. The sudden noise spooked her. When she looked out of the window, she saw a man lying in the snow near the tree that Cathy always had draped in outdoor lights for the festive season. By the deep tracks in the snow, she guessed that he had tripped over the low border of shrubs that marked the garden boundary and had fallen there.

In dismay she pulled on her friend's outdoor boots and jacket, pausing only to grab up the walking stick by the door because she knew she would struggle to get an injured man into the house without help. How long would it take for the emergency services to arrive in such weather? Where had he come from? He was dressed like a walker, but it was the hardly the season for hill walking.

In the act of trying to raise himself the man slumped down again, relieving her of the fear that he was unconscious.

'You'll freeze if you stay out in this.' Shivering, Lara shook his shoulder. 'Up!' she instructed in desperation. 'It'll take ages for anyone to come here and help and by then you might be dead from exposure.'

'You're a cheerful little soul,' her accident victim mumbled.

Relieved that he was at least well enough to be sarcastic, Lara grabbed a handful of the back of his jacket and tried to pull him, but he weighed a ton. 'Come on!' she urged.

'I hit my head…everything's spinning,' he framed.

'You can have the pity party indoors where it's warm.' Lara brushed away black tousled hair to whisper in his ear. 'Lovely fire, nice hot drink. Come on, I can't do this without your help.'

He groaned and started to raise himself again.

'Lean on me,' she told him, bending down and dragging his arm to her shoulder. 'Now... *move!*'

He moved, indeed got as far as his knees before *she* was driven face down into the snow by his weight.

Shaking herself free of snow, she rolled upright. 'Good, we're getting somewhere... you're halfway there.'

He blinked in bewilderment, snowflakes falling and clogging on the most outrageous curling black lashes. Dark, dark eyes, the kind that a woman stared at. It was Lara's turn to blink in puzzlement that such a thought should occur to her at such a time. Was she crazy?

'Here...use the stick as a support,' she pressed, pushing it into his hand, closing his clumsy fingers round it and standing. 'It's only a few yards.'

He levered himself up and swayed. 'Sick, dizzy.'

'Lean on me,' she advised, staggering when he obliged. 'Glory be, why do you have to be so big?'

'Why do you have to be so small?' he groaned, lurching forward at a snail's pace, his feet dragging. 'What height are you?'

'Four feet ten,' Lara admitted with great reluctance.

He staggered and swayed outside the back door, struggling to stay upright, and she thrust the door wide, scared to let go of him in case he went down again.

'Four feet ten,' he slurred like a drunk. 'Like a miniature person out of *Gulliver's Travels.*'

'Enough!' Lara snapped as he stumbled over the threshold and rocked like a very tall building in an earthquake. 'Over to the seat by the fire before you fall down.'

'Don't overheat me…it's dangerous with hypothermia,' he warned her.

Lara gritted her teeth as she guided his wavering steps towards the stove and pressed him down in the big fireside chair there. A sharp word from her silenced the mad excitement of the dogs careening round them. She swiped off his beanie because she had noticed a bloodstain on it and walked round to the back of the chair, tipping his head forward. He had a lot of dense black hair and she gently felt through it to feel the sizeable swelling there. There was no large wound and didn't seem to be any fresh blood. The rich musky scent of him assailed her nostrils. He smelled incredibly good.

'I think you'll live,' she murmured unevenly, still out of breath from her efforts with him. 'Are your feet wet?'

'*Sì...*'

The foreign word took her aback because he had previously spoken what she would have described as distinctly posh public-school English. 'Wet?' she pressed again.

'Yes,' he finally mumbled.

'We've got to take off anything wet that you're wearing to raise your temperature and then I'll get blankets.' Lara dropped down at his feet to tackle his boots. 'I thought these would have been waterproof.'

'Got my socks wet,' he groaned.

Lara rolled her eyes and dragged off the sodden socks, noting that he even had nicely shaped feet. She raced off to get blankets from Cathy's substantial airing cupboard. Returning to his side, she checked his waterproof jacket.

'Think we'd better get this off too…let the heat in,' she reasoned uncertainly, unzipping and unsnapping at speed.

'Are you planning to strip all of me?' he asked lazily, raising his head for the first time to look directly at her.

And, wow, that first glance froze her in her tracks because it was the first proper look she had managed to have of him, so busy had she been trying to get him into the house and then work out what best to do for him. Now the most amazing caramel-brown eyes collided with hers and held her fast. Looking away was more than she could contrive when those stunning eyes, illuminated to tawny gold by the firelight, were set in the most gorgeous masculine face. Tousled black hair tumbled over his brow to match sculpted cheekbones, an arrogant blade of a nose and a strong jawline, enhanced by a swirl of thick black stubble. His incredible bone structure was very distinctive and, she thought weakly, capable of turning any female head.

'You're like a doll,' he muttered, frowning and moving his head slightly to focus better, his lips compressing as she hovered in front of him.

'You're in pain.'

'Only a headache,' he parried, shifting his wide shoulders back and letting her tug at his sleeve to free one arm. As he spoke the dogs settled round his feet and their relaxed attitude to him eased her tension.

Lara dragged the jacket off and set it aside before checking the long-sleeved top he wore underneath. It was dry but she could feel the clammy chill of his broad chest underneath. And the realisation that she had been so busy mooning over him that she had momentarily forgotten what was most important shamed her. Shooing the dogs away, she grabbed up the blankets and carefully covered him, tucking the warm folds round his bare feet with extra care. To her amusement the dogs settled back round him again.

'I need to get you warm,' she muttered, stoking the stove to encourage a fresh burst of heat.

'It's a shame sharing body heat to chase the

cold has gone out of fashion,' he murmured sibilantly.

My goodness, he was flirting with her, so he couldn't be that injured, Lara registered in disconcertion, a flush warming her cheeks. She didn't have much practice with flirting. Decent men tended to assume she was younger than she was and treat her like a kid sister. The oversexed types wasted little time trying to get her into bed, which was a major turn-off for her. The men who she deemed attractive were invariably not attracted to her. That was why she was still a virgin at twenty-one. But that lack of sexual experience was also the result of her adoptive mother's frequent affairs and break-ups, not to mention the sleazy boyfriends who had targeted Lara as an adolescent. The way she saw it, a little restraint was an extra tool in her self-preservation box.

'You're very shy,' he mumbled thickly.

Seeing that his head was dipping lower, she shook herself free of his intoxicating effect on her and said anxiously, 'No, don't go to sleep. As far as I know you shouldn't be sleeping, not with the concussion you probably have.'

'Are you a nurse?'

'No, that's just basic first aid. I should ring for an ambulance now.'

'Don't need an ambulance, don't need medical attention. I got a knock on my head. It's no big deal.'

'Are you a doctor?'

'You're cheeky,' he sighed.

'Look, I'm going to phone the nearest neighbour for advice…she's a retired doctor. Please try and stay awake.' Dr Beresford, a keen craftswoman whom she had often met in Cathy's shop, would tell her whether or not she should call the emergency services to attend to her uninvited guest, although on such a night possibly only a tractor or a snowplough would manage to get up the road.

Moving out to the hall, she dug out her mobile phone to ring the woman.

Dr Beresford cut through her apologies for disturbing her. 'A walker?' she prompted in astonishment.

'Yes… I thought it was crazy in this weather too. He's hit his head and has a bump on the back of it but no other injuries. I'm trying to warm him up and I'll give him tea.'

'No stimulants,' the doctor warned her. 'Does he seem confused?'

'No. Aside of a headache he seems all right but he's pretty shaky on his feet.'

'If he's not seriously hurt it's unlikely that the emergency services would fly in to pick him up. I know for a fact that they're already dealing with a motorway pile-up this evening. But I don't like leaving you alone with a strange man either. Possibly if I were to inform the police or the mountain rescue team *they* would make the effort to walk up from—'

'That's not necessary,' Lara declared. 'He's not the creepy type…and I would know.'

'Well, that's good. I wish I could say that I could call over tomorrow but with Cathy's road in such a state—'

'I'll be fine. We've got heat and food. Should I be keeping him awake?'

Having received her instructions, Lara finished the call and walked back into the spacious kitchen and living area. Her uninvited visitor had fallen asleep while the dogs snored at his feet. She decided to leave him in peace until she had made a pot of tea and some ham sandwiches. While the kettle boiled, she studied him. He really was quite ridiculously handsome, she mused, no longer embarrassed by her previous reaction to him. She was convinced that any woman would have found herself staring just a little too long at such perfect masculine features. Entirely symmetrical features, eyelashes long enough to trip on and a superbly shaped pale pink mouth set in an extensive black shadow of stubble. His deep voice, the angular strength of his jaw and his sheer size lent him a ferociously masculine quality and yet even when he had flirted with her just a little there had been nothing to creep her out.

And nobody knew more about creepy men than Lara did. Her mother had had several live-in boyfriends who liked very young girls: men with sleazy eyes who tracked her every move once her skinny body began to develop petite curves, men who got too friendly when her mother was absent, men whose hands strayed where they shouldn't, men who hovered in her bedroom doorway saying, 'Just checking on you…'

With a shiver of recollection, Lara shot out of that last frightening memory and lifted the tray to carry it over to the coffee table. Leaning forward, she gave his shoulder a slight shake to wake him as gently as possible before sitting down again.

'Dr Beresford said to only let you sleep for small stretches. I'll wake you up every couple of hours to check that you're all right.'

'Oh, joy,' he drawled softly.

'Yes, I'm looking forward to a night without much sleep too,' Lara countered gently, determined not to take any nonsense. 'It'll be rather like having a baby in the house.'

Her visitor stared back at her in disbelief.

'Do you take sugar and milk in your tea?'

'Milk, yes…sugar, no. But I don't *drink* tea,' he told her. 'I only drink coffee… I think,' he completed, less certainly, his voice trailing off as his brow furrowed as if something was confusing him.

'But coffee is a stimulant and the doctor advised against that.'

'Do we have to follow even the tiniest piece of medical advice?'

'Yes,' Lara confirmed. 'As long as you're my responsibility.'

'I'm not sure I want to be anyone's responsibility,' he framed tautly.

He didn't like being told no, didn't like restrictions, was possibly even accustomed to his looks and charisma smoothing his path in life. Lara smiled and shrugged. She poured tea into a mug and set it close to him. 'I made sandwiches. I don't know if you're hungry.'

He sipped the tea with a wince of distaste that he tried really hard to hide. He was arrogant but he had manners, she decided. She offered him the plate of sandwiches. He accepted one and she smiled again, thinking that an appetite was a healthy sign.

'I'm Lara, Lara Drummond,' she murmured.

'Lara…that's unusual,' he remarked rather than responding as she had expected with his own name.

'You can blame my mother. She was a big fan of *Dr Zhivago*.'

He gave her a blank look and she settled the sandwich plate in front of him.

'It's a film set in Russia during the first world war, starring Julie Christie and Omar Sharif,' Lara explained ruefully, because it was obvious that he didn't know what she was talking about. 'It's a romantic drama. That's where I got my name from.'

'Are you romantic?'

'Not at all.' Lara rolled her eyes at that idea

after the adolescent experiences she had enjoyed. 'What's your name?'

'Guy…' he responded instantly and then he went oddly stiff and closed his lips again, his brows drawing together in a frown.

'Guy.' It struck her as an upper-class name that was a perfect match for his posh accent. He wasn't very talkative. Of course, it could just be that he wasn't feeling well and that he was exhausted, she scolded herself as she pushed another sandwich at him, keen to drive the frown from his lean dark features.

'And you got lost,' she commented.

'Yes,' he confirmed in an odd tone of finality. 'I think I saw the tree with lights just before I fell. It feels familiar…somehow.'

'Cathy loves to put the lights out on the apple tree so that she can see it from her kitchen window.'

'Cathy?' he queried.

'The owner of the house. Well, Cathy and her husband, Brian. This is their home.'

'And who are you?'

'The house-sitter…an unofficial one. Cathy and Brian are spending Christmas in Australia and I'm here looking after everything until they come home,' she clarified. 'Let me show you to your room…'

He stood up slowly and his lashes flickered as he shifted his shoulders and his neck with caution.

'Luckily there's a room down here that you can use. I can see you're still a bit dizzy so it's best you don't tackle the stairs yet. The room's small but it's comfortable,' she confided, pushing open the door, relieved to see that the bed was already made up and that she wouldn't have to do it.

'Is there a bathroom?'

'Yes, but I'm not sure you should use the shower yet either.'

'I have a headache but that's it,' he said firmly as she opened another door across the corridor to indicate the washing facilities.

'I'll be in the kitchen. I'm going to use the sofa tonight so that I can stay within reach.'

His curling black lashes dipped low over his dark eyes, and he flashed her a slow-burning smile of appreciation that made her heart thunder in her ears and her mouth run dry. 'I appreciate all the help you've given me. Thank you.'

She stood in the hallway a full minute

after he had vanished into the bathroom and then her brain kicked in again and moved her. But that smile of his, my goodness when his whole face lit up like that he was stunning. Returning to the kitchen, she tidied up, tended to the animals and settled them for the night. Shortly after that she heard Guy close the bedroom door and she expelled her breath on a hiss.

Who was he? Why hadn't she asked him where his stuff had gone? Had he lost it in the snow when he fell? Or had he simply been out rambling? If so, he could only be staying somewhere within reasonable reach but there were no houses closer than Dr Beresford's and even she was a couple of miles away. And if he did have accommodation nearby, why hadn't he mentioned it? Her own head was starting to ache with stress, and she went upstairs, donned her warmest pyjamas, gathered up her duvet and her alarm clock and went back downstairs to get as comfy as she could on the sofa.

The alarm wakened her from a solid sleep, and it took a moment or two for her to orientate herself and recall why she was getting up in the middle of the night. Sighing, she clambered off the sofa. She felt a bit cruel waking him up after the experience he had been through, and she brought him a warm drink as a consolation. She knocked on the bedroom door and waited but there was no sound within. Compressing her lips, she went in, the light from the hallway illuminating the room. She set the drink on the bedside cabinet.

He was fast asleep, his black hair very dark against the pale bedding. She bent down, steadying herself with one hand on the headboard, and shook the arm resting on top of the duvet. 'Guy?' she prompted. 'It's time to wake up…'

He stretched up a hand and found her shoulder, his dark eyes flying wide in surprise. '*Mi dispiace*…what did you say?' he framed groggily.

'I brought you a warm drink. How are you feeling?'

He slid a leg out of bed and began to rise, making her suddenly aware of how very tall he was. She stumbled backwards. As he lifted his hands as though to reassure her and stay her retreat, he caught his foot in the trailing duvet and lurched forward, knocking her off balance. A gasp of dismay parted Lara's lips as she went crashing down on the floor with him on top of her. They looked at each other, stunned by the accident, and then just as quickly Lara began to shake with giggles.

'*Mi dispiace,*' he said again.

'What does that mean?' Lara asked, her aquamarine eyes brimming with laughter at their mutual clumsiness.

'I'm sorry… I am truly sorry,' he declared, struggling to disentangle his foot from the bedding.

'It was your expression…the shock and horror!' she gasped, giggles convulsing her again.

'Stop,' he told her, raising himself up from her prone body to release her from his weight.

He was smiling now though, his shapely mouth quirking with reluctant amusement, his dark golden eyes alight as he scanned her triangular face.

'You are shockingly cute and sexy,' he muttered.

Her eyes brightened even more. 'Seriously?'

'Even in Christmas pudding pyjamas,' he conceded in unhidden wonderment, his mouth drifting down closer to hers. '*Dancing* Christmas puddings too…'

Lara couldn't breathe that close to him, but she lifted her head up to him, eyes wide, lips parting in an invitation that seemed so natural in that moment.

His breath fanned her cheek, his lips brushed hers in the briefest possible caress and a feverish little shiver of delicious response rippled through her. With a groan, he levered back from her, and she followed him by sitting up, eyes starry as she stared at him.

'This is crazy,' he breathed.

Rebellion twisted inside Lara, who had learned to repress her secret desires and always do the sensible thing. Every time, she did the sensible thing…until she leant forward quite deliberately, all tantalising, teasing femininity, and their mouths collided. It was as if one of them had struck a match and lit a firework as he eased her gently towards him and kissed her with all the unrestrained passion she had always craved and never once received from a man. The pressure of his mouth on hers was urgent, demanding, igniting a new and irresistible hunger. She had never felt that way before and she kissed him back with enthusiasm, squirming with pleasure as his tongue stroked along hers. A flood of heat surged between her thighs, her nipples prickling into tight little buds.

'Really crazy,' he extended gruffly, carefully setting her back from him and using the bed to haul himself upright again.

Only then did she become aware that he was only wearing boxers that moulded every angle of his big muscular bronzed body and the effect of that kiss on him was fairly obvious. She reddened, seized by the awful heat of embarrassment at how forward she had been. Such behaviour was so out of character for her that she was astonished by it. The ache that had stirred at the heart of her tightened, reminding her of its presence. Red as a beetroot, she scrambled upright.

'Don't know what happened there. I brought you a hot chocolate,' she muttered in a rush, indicating the mug. 'How do you feel?'

'Lousy,' he groaned, settling back on the bed and yanking up the duvet to cover himself. 'I don't think my name is Guy. It doesn't feel familiar.'

Lara was taken aback. 'But you *said* your name was Guy.'

'No. I began to say the name but when I thought about it, it wasn't there any more in my head.' He sighed. 'I'd forgotten it like everything else.'

Her eyes full of concern, Lara hovered. 'Like everything else?'

Guy, who wasn't sure he *was* Guy, studied her. 'I can't remember *anything*. My name, what I was doing out there in the snow alone… who I am…where I come from…there's just this great woolly blank inside my head!' he exclaimed in a frustrated undertone.

Emotion boiled like swirling dark water in his highly expressive eyes and nothing could have masked the hint of panic edging his low voice. Lara winced. 'You banged your head. You're confused and, if you can't remember now, it'll probably all come back to you by morning. The worst thing you can do is get upset about it.'

'Of course, I'm upset about it!' he exclaimed rawly.

'And the more upset you are about it, the more confused you will feel. Try and get some sleep now,' she urged quietly and swiftly moved back to the door.

'I shouldn't have kissed you,' he breathed abruptly. 'It was inappropriate and I apologise.'

'It was nothing, a mad thoughtless moment…that's all,' Lara replied with forced lightness of tone. 'Anyway, I did encourage you and I didn't exactly run away screaming.'

'Nonetheless—'

'Leave it there. Calm your mind and rest.'

'What am I going to do if I don't remember by morning?' he groaned.

'We'll see.'

What on earth had she done? Kissing him like that when he was half naked and she was wearing her stupid festive pyjamas? Lara slid back under her duvet and shivered with cold and shock. She hadn't known a man could make you feel like that with a kiss. She hadn't known she *could* feel like that. Only a kiss though, she reminded herself tiredly, don't make a silly fuss about a kiss…

CHAPTER THREE

Present day

LARA SHOOK OFF those memories in haste as she changed to meet up with Gaetano. She saw no reason why she should show up bare-faced and wearing her oldest jeans, looking as though she had given up on even trying to be attractive. No, she wasn't ready to be seen in that light, not when *he* was dressed and groomed as if he were about to walk into an expensive restaurant or a fancy business meeting!

As soon as she had Freddy tucked into his sleeping bag clutching his beloved toy rabbit she went for a shower and washed her hair. She had to raid Alice's cosmetics to do her face. She grimaced. She hadn't given up after her marriage imploded before her eyes, she *hadn't*! But she had had no interest in men after that humiliation and then, in no time at all, she had discovered that she was pregnant. And Freddy's arrival had changed everything. Her years of evening classes aimed at helping her catch up on the education she had missed out on had counted for nothing once she'd had to work out how to survive on her own and provide for her son as well.

Alice had saved her life by offering her a home and the two women had fallen into a comfortable groove, working around each other and sharing childcare. But Lara had had few choices when it came to how she made her living. She worked at night cleaning commercial premises because those hours of work suited her. Freddy was in bed and although Alice had to babysit, she wasn't actively having to do much. Lara operated on less sleep and contrived to spend most of her day with her son and slot Iris, who was at school, into their schedule as well. The arrangement suited both women for the present even if it didn't allow scope for Lara to aspire to more rewarding employment. That could wait until Freddy was at school and she had the freedom to consider other options. Currently, Lara worked sufficient hours to ensure that rent, food and other basic needs were covered without her having to take too much advantage of Alice's frequently offered generosity.

Having put on her dressiest outfit while scolding herself for putting so much effort into her appearance, Lara slotted her feet into perilously high heels. Alice had bought them for her the previous Christmas, mainly as a joke, saying that it was time Lara went out and painted the town red with her. Only that one night out being hit on by men who neither attracted nor interested her had put Lara off and persuaded her that she was far too picky. Nor did the idea of having to explain her marital situation appeal to her. Being possibly married without a husband left her in a kind of no man's land when it came to dating and she knew she needed to do something about that.

'You look incredible. I gather you want him to regret how he treated you?'

'It's a bit late in the day for that,' Lara contended. 'But that doesn't mean I want him to look at me and feel that his worst expectations of me have been vindicated, which I'm sure is exactly what he thought when he took me by surprise today in the park.'

Alice handed her the keys for the hatchback parked in the drive. Lara slipped off the shoes and drove off. Her heart was sitting at the base of her throat. She just couldn't credit that she was about to see Gaetano again. That brief encounter in the park already had the unreal hazy edge of a dream. No, not a dream, she decided ruefully, a nightmare. What woman wanted to lay eyes on the man who had broken her heart again? Gaetano di Santis had ripped her in two, but she wasn't the same trusting and vulnerable woman that she had been. She lifted her chin. *Game on, Gaetano!*

The satellite navigation led her to a stately home situated in its own park. Of course, he would hardly be slumming it, not a king, not a male born into generations of royalty and the luxury lifestyle that went with such status. She drove down the long winding driveway, staring at the imposing façade of the large Victorian mansion and wincing. Immediately she felt underdressed and out of her comfort zone. Stiffening her spine while telling herself off for being so sensitive, she put on her shoes, locked the car and walked across the gravel very slowly to the pillared entrance, striving not to totter in her high heels.

Two men in suits greeted her at the door and asked her who she was visiting.

'Gaetano,' she said tightly, colour lacing her pallor at having to make even that much of an explanation, and their surprised looks didn't help.

'His Majesty is working in the library,' one of them whispered to the other, their low-pitched voices seemingly part of their job.

'His Majesty doesn't like to be disturbed unnecessarily,' another voice, which was female, interposed brightly from the rear of the hall. 'Perhaps I can help?'

Lara glanced at the svelte blonde older woman, unimpressed by her welcoming smile when her blue eyes were as hard as granite. 'I don't think so…possibly I should've called ahead.'

'That would have been wise. Perhaps you could phone and make an appointment first. Usually that approach works best with some-one as busy as the King,' the woman pointed out cuttingly.

Lara walked back outside, dug out her phone and the card Gaetano had given her to punch in the number. 'Gaetano?' she asked as soon as it was answered. 'I'm outside and ready to head home again. I can't get past your staff. I'll give you a count of ten before I leave.'

Lara strolled back towards the car. As she unlocked the door a lion's roar broke the evening silence. *'Lara!'*

Gaetano now stood in the porch in person, seething annoyance emanating from him in a wave, a touch of colour accentuating his high cheekbones.

'I should've phoned and told you what time I would be here *before* I left home,' Lara conceded gracefully as she walked back towards him, barely able to breathe above the nervous tension gripping her chest in a vice. 'But I wasn't expecting all this security.'

His intense dark gaze burned over her to the extent that she almost stumbled over her own feet in the grand hall.

'Allow me to take your coat,' a little man proffered, extending his hands.

Lara doffed the black wool coat she usually only wore for church, and it was carried off with the same reverence that a fantastically expensive designer garment would have commanded. Under Gaetano's incredulous scrutiny the floral dress that swirled round her knees suddenly felt incredibly tight and she shifted her feet uneasily.

Gaetano studied her fixedly. In any terminology his wife was a living, breathing doll with delicate flawless features. She was tiny and shapely with perfect legs, porcelain-pale skin and a wealth of wavy strawberry-blonde hair tumbling round her narrow shoulders. She looked amazing, not a thought that he believed he should be having in such circumstances, but it was, at least, the proof that he had not been entirely insane two years earlier when he'd promised to marry her and forsake all others. As if in evidence of his susceptibility as he noted the luscious peach of her mouth and the surprisingly full curve of her small breasts, a warning pulse throbbed at his groin and he tensed, infuriated by that response. Was that reaction really so surprising when he was sex-starved?

'What on earth are you wearing on your feet?' Gaetano demanded abruptly. 'All of a sudden you're unnaturally tall!'

Lara extended bare toes cradled in clear plastic straps, her heel raised a towering six

inches by the sandal. She tilted her chin.
'Why not?' she said lightly. She had a choice
of trainers, a pair of biker boots and the silly
sandals. There were few options in Lara's
slender wardrobe. She didn't go out much
and she didn't need many outfits.

'Let's go into the library,' another voice
slotted in quietly.

Lara froze, uneasily conscious of being
the cynosure of every eye around them. An
alien dropping in could not have commanded
more attention. The security men were standing at the back, frowning. The sharp-tongued
blonde was staring a perplexed hole in her.
She shot a glance at the lean bearded man
she recalled from two years earlier, Gaetano's
protective sidekick, as she had tagged him.
She tasted bile in her mouth. He was a lawyer
and a personal friend. She didn't remember
his name, but she did remember his shocked
and hostile attitude to her.

'I'm here to see you *alone*,' Lara told
Gaetano defensively.

'That's not a problem,' he responded
smoothly, ignoring the frown of disapproval
from his friend.

The butler, who had borne off her coat,

moved forward to guide her into a side corridor and usher her into a heavily furnished
Victorian library. Gaetano stepped past her
and lounged back against the side of the desk,
which had an open laptop on it.

'This meeting is difficult for both of us
because so much time has passed,' Gaetano
remarked smoothly. 'Did it not occur to you
that I would need to get in touch with you?'

His cool composure bit into Lara like a
blade. Inside herself she was a mess of pain
and regret. She was looking at the man she
had loved, and he hadn't had the decency to
develop a pot belly and a receding hairline
to banish her idealised memories. No, he had
got even more gorgeous in a scarily sleek, sophisticated way. He wasn't the guy with the
tousled black hair, stubble and jeans whom
she had fallen head over heels for within days.
He wasn't the guy looking to her for understanding and support when he was suddenly
thrown into an unfamiliar world. He wasn't
the man whom she had taught to cook and
wield an axe, marvelling at his lack of ordinary practical knowledge. No, this was a guy
wearing an exquisitely tailored navy suit that
probably cost more than she'd earned in two

years of work. His hair was perfectly styled, his jawline clean-shaven, his dark blue shirt perfectly complemented by his silver tie. The only thing she had remembered right about the guy she'd married was that he was very, *very* good-looking.

'I wasn't thinking about stuff of that nature when I left,' Lara replied flatly.

She had run in pain and humiliation as if she could somehow leave that horrible sense of rejection behind her if she ran fast enough. She had run as an animal ran, without thought or consideration. Too late she had learned that pain found you wherever you ran and that there was no escaping it.

'It has taken me all this time to track you down,' Gaetano informed her.

Was he expecting an apology? Lara gritted her small white teeth, knowing she hadn't wanted to be found, not when it entailed standing in front of Gaetano as if she were being hauled over the coals for some dreadful mistake. Quite deliberately she settled into an armchair without being asked, sneering at her foolish younger self for not guessing from the first that such comfort and opulence was Gaetano's natural milieu. His confidence, his innate good manners, his ability to speak more than one language and wide-ranging general knowledge. All those facts should have made her appreciate that his position in society was far removed from hers. She truly hadn't thought such things as class mattered any more. But Gaetano had taught her different when he'd looked at the not-very-well-educated waitress he had chosen to marry and make his. In shock and dismay and regret.

'I wasn't even sure we *were* legally married,' she pointed out defensively.

Gaetano frowned. 'Why would you think we were not?'

A tight little laugh was wrenched from Lara. 'Don't you remember what Dario said that day? He said something about constitutional law and how could you get legally married without the sovereign's consent? So, obviously I thought that the legality of our marriage was in doubt.'

'That wasn't the case. There *is* no such law relating to the royal family in Mosvakia.' Gaetano clenched his teeth, knocked off topic by that admission of hers because he remembered little of what had been said that morning. He had been reeling with shock and grief.

At one and the same time he had regained his memory and learned that his brother had died, and he was now King.

Lara nodded in silence.

'Now that you're here, however, I do see that it is best to make this encounter impersonal.'

'Impersonal?' Lara almost whispered, crossing her legs in the hope that he wouldn't realise her lower limbs were shaking. How the heck could a divorce be deemed impersonal?

A knock sounded on the door and the little man who had taken her coat appeared with a laden tray. There was much bowing and scraping in Gaetano's direction before the tray finally reached the side table and they were alone again.

Gaetano cleared his throat. '*Sì*, impersonal. After this length of time, nothing else makes sense. There should be no recriminations, no bad feelings.'

What had happened to the passionate guy who had swept her off her feet and insisted on marrying her after a mere ten days of acquaintance?

'I doubt if that is possible, but I have no

wish to get into an argument with you,' Lara declared stiffly.

'We've been living apart for two years and all I require is your consent on a document to a divorce. That consent, while not strictly necessary, would make the proceedings run more smoothly.' As Gaetano spoke, he tapped a document and pen lying on the desk. 'May I ask my friend and lawyer, Dario Rossi, to join us?'

'No,' Lara said succinctly, still unable to overcome her aversion to the man who had viewed her with cool hostility while her entire world had caved in round her ears, all his concern reserved for Gaetano. And back then, Gaetano *had* been her whole world because she had never even dared to dream of finding a love like that and, having found it, she had been devastated when it had proved to be an empty illusion.

'No?' Gaetano queried in polite surprise.

'No,' Lara repeated. 'I didn't take to him at our first meeting.'

Gaetano surveyed her, noticing that she hadn't poured the coffee and marvelling at her seeming tranquillity, which was why her refusal to allow Dario to join them took him aback. She seemed as though she were a thousand miles away from him inside her head and he hadn't expected that air of emotional detachment from her, not from a woman he remembered as being wonderfully warm and caring.

'Do you have any objection to us getting divorced?' he intoned flatly.

Lara gritted her teeth again. 'No,' she asserted.

'Let me assure you that I will pay all your legal fees to the lawyer of your choice. There will also be a substantial financial settlement,' Gaetano informed her, getting back into his stride again.

'I don't want your money,' Lara told him, wondering when he was planning to get around to mentioning Freddy and also wondering if she was cutting off her nose to spite her face, as her grandmother would have quipped. After all, money would allow her to get her life in order sooner than she had hoped and build towards a better future.

'I owe you some compensation for the way our relationship played out,' Gaetano countered gravely. 'But I do also wish to thank you for the valuable assistance you gave me during the weeks we were together. Matters could have gone a great deal less pleasantly for me.'

'I wish I'd left you in the snow!' Lara retorted, and even as she made that childish statement she knew she was lying because without Gaetano, there would be no Freddy and Lara's life revolved around Freddy.

'I don't believe that.'

Her huge aquamarine eyes that were neither blue nor green and changed according to her mood flashed at him, but she compressed her lips and remained silent.

'Would you like coffee?' Gaetano was finally moved to ask in the smouldering silence. He felt curiously reluctant to let her go. On some level, he simply wanted to feast his eyes on her because, aside of the absurd shoes, she was every bit as beautiful and sexy as he recalled. He recalled other things about her as well, things he tried to bury but that often returned to him when he was alone. The way she smiled when the sun shone, the way she reached for him in the darkness, the way she laughed when he said something she deemed silly or unrealistic. And a whole host of other far more sexual recollections such as what it felt like when her tiny body clenched round his in climax, how shy she got in daylight, the ridiculous inhibitions about time, place and frequency she had harboured in the field of intimacy.

Recognising the heat building below his belt, Gaetano had cause to be grateful for the concealment of his suit jacket. Yes, she still turned him on, turned him on more than other women, but he had to walk away from that kind of temptation and do his duty. He had to have a wife and children. That he hadn't been trained to accept that sacrifice wasn't an excuse. The responsibility that had once been Vittorio's was now his and there was no point complaining about it. In the most basic sense, producing the next generation with an acceptable woman lay at the very heart of his role as monarch.

'No, thanks. I'm not staying.' Indeed, Lara was already rising from her seat, eager to be gone.

Her cheeks were pink, her striking eyes downcast as she disconcerted him by reaching for the pen and scrawling her signature on the document that Dario had given him.

'You shouldn't sign a legal document without your own lawyer at hand to represent your interests,' Gaetano remarked tautly.

'That's your world, not mine,' Lara parried in a tone of scorn. 'I don't require a lawyer to tell me I want to be free of you. You have disappointed me in every conceivable way, Gaetano.'

'I regret that you feel that way,' he breathed curtly.

'No, your only goal is that I sign this form so that you can shed any responsibility you might have for me as discreetly as possible. That doesn't surprise me but I'm angry on my *son's* behalf!' Lara countered, throwing her head back. 'He is an innocent party here and you didn't even *look* at him at the park!'

'You're trying to say that your son is also… *my* son?' Gaetano framed in open disbelief.

'He's sixteen months old, Gaetano. Who else could be his father?' she fired at him in disgust. 'But don't worry, we're getting along fine without you and we need nothing from you. Even so, your lack of even polite interest in him is unforgivable!'

With that ringing indictment of his attitude, Lara dealt him a seething look of condemnation and stalked out of the room, down the corridor and into the hall. 'My coat?' she urged with an edge of desperation when the little manservant appeared.

Pulling her coat on, she stomped down the steps and across to the car. Her mobile began ringing. She ignored it and knew she would block his calls. She didn't want to exchange another word with Gaetano. She was too angry with him and too hurt by his indifference to their son…

CHAPTER FOUR

THE FOLLOWING MORNING, Dario was talking in legal mode, a habit that often led to Gaetano beginning to tune him out while on one level he continued to listen without engaging. They were both in shock but while his friend reacted as a lawyer, Gaetano was reacting as a man who had just learned that he might be a father. His brain was in a state of freefall because Lara's claim had shattered him.

How could he have a child he didn't know about?

How could Mosvakia have a crown prince it had yet to learn existed?

Why the hell hadn't Lara told him that she was pregnant? He should have been involved from the start. He should have been there at the birth of his child, and it galled him that he had been denied that right and all the other rights that fatherhood bestowed.

'You didn't even think there was a possibility that the child could be yours?'

'The investigation agency assumed the child was older and that misled me,' Gaetano murmured, refusing to elucidate on that topic further. 'We should have waited until the birth certificate was available.'

'You will need DNA tests.' Dario was not to be silenced. 'Had I known there was the possibility that the boy could be your heir I would have advised a very different kind of approach to the mother.'

Gaetano gazed out of the window, impervious to the view. 'I didn't realise conception could be that easy. I watched Vittorio and Giulia struggle for years trying to have a child, going through all that fertility treatment...' His shapely mouth compressed, and he said no more about his brother's misfortunes in that department. But his visceral response to the concept of being a father and of that being a huge honour as well as a life-changing responsibility was steadily increasing.

His mother had abandoned him as a toddler and hadn't even thought better of that move when only months later his father was killed in a car crash. To all intents and purposes,

Vittorio had become his half-brother's father as a twenty-year old. Even at that young age, Vittorio had made a real effort to be a parent to the lonely child in the royal nursery and Gaetano had loved him accordingly. Recalling that truth, Gaetano swore that he would do no less for his own child and, hopefully, he would do a great deal more bearing in mind that he was older and wiser.

'I *must* see him!' he exclaimed abruptly. 'How can I not even know my son's name?'

'You shouldn't rush into anything before there's proof.'

'Dario, stop being a lawyer,' Gaetano interrupted with a frown. 'How would you feel if you discovered you were a father purely by accident? What if I hadn't searched for Lara? What if I hadn't been able to track her down? I might *never* have known I had a son!'

'In your position, I'd hang her out to dry for this,' Dario countered. 'I understand your anger.'

Gaetano almost groaned out loud at that response. He wanted to see his child, but Lara appeared to have blocked his number. He suspected that Lara was endeavouring to ignore the destruction she had wreaked and remained in denial. *He* had disappointed *her*? Why didn't she turn that around and accept how much she had disappointed *him*?

By that evening with his patience running out, Gaetano chose to ignore Dario's dire warnings and he called in person at Lara's home. The door was opened by her friend. She was very respectful but firm in her certainty that she could not allow him to see his child without Lara's presence. Gaetano cursed the fact that he had forgotten that Lara worked nights. He rang Dario to get him to look up the file and get him the name of the cleaning firm.

'This is not discreet, sir,' Dario lamented in a studiously formal manner.

Gaetano ground his teeth together. He was *done* with discretion. He rarely lost his temper but there was a knot of rage gradually tightening inside him. That rage had had twenty-four hours to grow. Lara had stolen his child from him, deprived him of his paternal rights and denied his son the benefit of a father. For what reason would he tolerate such treatment?

'I'll be out of your way in five minutes,' the last office occupant on the floor informed Lara without even looking at her.

And cleaning while being ignored by those who did overtime was exactly how Lara preferred to work. She had learned that it was best to melt into the woodwork. Her hair was concealed by a beanie, her overall baggy enough to conceal any hint of the shape of the female body inside it. The last thing she wanted was male attention when she was alone in an almost empty office block. Her unwelcome experiences in that line from her years living with her adoptive mother had made her very cautious around men.

As the man departed, leaving her free to empty the rubbish bin and run a mop across the floor, she donned her ear buds. Soon she was humming beneath her breath while planning what she would do to keep Freddy amused the next day. Just letting him pelt round the house didn't work. He was a lively, demanding child, better kept occupied than allowed to get bored.

Gaetano strode down the corridor of the anonymous office block where his wife worked...*cleaning*. Did she enjoy being a martyr? Saying she didn't want or need his money when she was forced to do such lowly work to survive? Putting *him* in the wrong even though she had deserted him and lost herself so very efficiently? When he saw her bent down in the office, he could not initially believe that that tiny amorphous figure was Lara. She looked like a homeless person rather than a young, attractive woman. She hadn't noticed him because she was too busy listening to music and how safe was that for a woman on her own in such a place?

And then even as he thought that Lara whirled round and almost leapt in the air in fright, the hand on the mop loosening its grip and letting it drop with a clatter against the bucket as she pressed her palm against her heart instead.

'What on earth…?' she gasped breathlessly, studying him with wide disbelieving eyes.

Such exotic eyes too: the aquamarine colour of the Adriatic Sea that washed the shore of Mosvakia, that indescribable peacock-blue-green shade that he had never seen in any other face. The very first thing he had noticed about her.

'How the heck did you find me? How the hell did you even get past the security guard at the entrance?' Lara hissed furiously.

'You blocked me on your phone. Did you

expect me to take that lying down?' Gaetano raked at her.

Lara dragged her beanie off with an exasperated hand, her face hot with embarrassment that he had chosen to ambush her during her cleaning shift. Wildly tossed strawberry waves fell round her shoulders and she pushed them angrily back behind her ears. 'I'm not having a fight with you, Gaetano, not here where I'm supposed to be working. I'll see you tomorrow when I am available. I am *not* available right now!'

As he stood in the office doorway, sheathed in a black cashmere overcoat and a dark grey suit teamed with a red shirt and a blue silk tie, Gaetano slashed a silencing hand in the air. It was, for Lara, a disturbingly regal and commanding gesture such as she had never seen from him before and it rather intimidated her.

'I don't care,' he shot at her. 'Last night you told me that I had a son and you seemed surprised that I didn't look at him in the park. I didn't know that he could *be* my son! And if he *is* my son, I don't even know his name!'

Lara folded her lips into a flat line. 'Naturally, since you tracked me down to the level of knowing *when* I went to the park, I assumed you also knew about him.'

'I flew out here the instant I had an address for you. The detective agency had not completed the report. I was told that there was a child, but he was estimated as several months older and I assumed that he wasn't mine.'

'Oh, for goodness' sake, Gaetano…how could he be anything *other* than yours when you were my first lover?' Lara derided in angry dismissal of that explanation. 'Keep your comforting self-delusions to yourself! I will not be insulted by that kind of insinuation because you want to put our marriage behind you as if it never happened!'

Gaetano's dark eyes were now burnished by a fiery glitter, his lean darkly handsome face still taut with tension. 'What is his name?' he asked rawly.

'Frederick. I named him after my grandfather, but I call him Freddy,' she admitted grudgingly. 'I'm afraid you're not named on the birth certificate.'

Another spear of anger pierced Gaetano's tough hide. He felt almost as though he had been written out of existence and their marriage with it. He stalked closer to her, his dark brooding gaze intense. 'Did you even think about what you were doing? About the legalities of lying on such a score? You are not allowed to rewrite my son's ancestry and deny him his father just because it suited you to do so. That is not your choice to make.'

'I thought you would want his ancestry hidden,' Lara argued helplessly, taken aback by his vehement objections. 'You didn't want me as a wife...why would you have wanted a child with me?'

'Mannaggia!' Gaetano vented in sheer frustration, barely able to cope with his loss of temper because he had been trained in childhood never ever to lose his temper. His wild tantrums as a young child had appalled his big brother. 'We will not discuss that statement here and now,' he bit out in a roughened undertone. 'But you must see that, even were the first statement to be true—and I'm not saying it *is*—the two things are not the same.'

Lara gathered up her equipment, stacked it noisily on her cleaning trolley and moved to the next office beneath his incredulous scrutiny, which made it clear that he could not credit that she could dare to continue with her job in his presence. 'No, I don't see or accept that,' she finally replied and got stuck into her job again.

She refused to give an inch to his expectations. He might be a king but he was not *her* king. Good grief, had she broken the law when she registered her son as a single woman and claimed that she did not know the father's name? She hadn't thought about stuff of that nature during her pregnancy when her only driving motivation had been to hide and ensure that nobody found out she had ever been foolish enough to marry an amnesiac, who had turned out to be so much more than she could ever have suspected. A dark horse, indeed. And the instant Gaetano had remembered *who* he was and *what* he was, he had spurned her. Her pained ruminations as she mopped the floor in rigid silence brought her right up to the very toes of his polished and, she was certain, highly expensive shoes.

'Stop this,' Gaetano bit out savagely. 'Stop trying to ignore me! I'm not going to go away. I am a very persistent, very determined man.'

'And I am a very angry, very bitter woman,' Lara snapped, still without looking at him.

Without warning, Gaetano lifted her off

her feet and deposited her gently on the side of a desk. The mop had fallen out of her hands with a clatter. 'That must be my fault, then, *bambola*,' he breathed with regret, sharply disconcerting her. 'You were not an angry, bitter woman when I met you...'

That truthful point released her fierce tension, and she was startled by the surge of prickling tears that hit the backs of her eyes because she was not a cry baby either. *Bambola*...doll...his pet name for her, a name she had believed she would never hear again, and it unleashed an anguished flood of memories inside her that hurt. 'Go away...' she told him shakily.

Gaetano trailed a fingertip across the single tear that had spilt down her cheek. 'I'm sorry I lost my temper and raised my voice.'

'We're not the same people we were two years ago.'

Gaetano almost said something sarcastic and bit it back just in time, suddenly struggling for *her* sake to be the man he had been before he got his memory back. He regretted the fact that that humbled, more hesitant version of himself had probably been far kinder and more considerate than he was, in reality.

'I don't want to hurt your feelings or you in any way,' he declared in a driven undertone. 'That's not why I'm here.'

'You're here for a divorce,' she reminded him unnecessarily.

'You sound like Dario. I don't need that right now,' Gaetano admitted with an honesty he hadn't observed in two long years, and the minute he uttered the words he wanted to bite them back because, until she had come into his life, he had never ever admitted a vulnerable moment to anyone, even his late brother.

Seated on the desk, she could not evade his eyes any longer. And for a split second she glimpsed the guy she had loved in the brooding turmoil of his beautiful dark eyes, and it anchored her a bit, made her feel more in control. She studied his lush black lashes, the perfect line of his nose, his shapely mouth in the sea of dark stubble that was beginning to shadow his jawline, and all of a sudden he seemed achingly familiar and her heart was clenching inside her chest again as though he had squeezed it.

He bent and lifted the fallen mop to set it out of his path, his distaste for the item unhidden.

'It's just a job!' she protested as if he had spoken, reading his body language with an ease that made him feel oddly naked because nobody did that around him, absolutely nobody.

'It's a job you don't *need* and that's one reason why I became angry,' Gaetano murmured fiercely. 'I am a very rich man and there is no need for you to be employed.'

'Gaetano—'

Gaetano made an exasperated zipping motion near her mouth with his finger, and she leant forward and nipped his fingertip lightly between her teeth in rebuke. It was something only Lara would do, and he couldn't help it, he grinned and burst out laughing, all annoyance vanquished.

A little embarrassed that she had got that personal, Lara lifted her flushed face and said, 'Well, you know I can't *stand* that mansplaining thing you do when you get all serious and pompous and talk like I haven't got a brain.'

'And you will naturally agree with me that you don't need to take a job from someone who does need it to make a point. You don't need money to survive, not with me around,' he instructed, clearly not having learned his lesson yet.

'But you're not around and we're getting a divorce.'

'Forget that. As your husband I am still responsible for keeping you and my child. Quit the job here and now,' he told her.

'I can't do that. I have notice to work if I want to leave.'

Gaetano groaned out loud. 'OK, strip this back to its most basic. If our marital situation gets into the media, I don't want to be the king with a wife scrubbing floors because he is too stingy to pay his dues,' he spelled out.

'You think it might get into the press about us?' she gasped in a panicked tone.

'I can assure you that my staff will do everything possible to keep us out of the newspapers, but we can't control everything,' Gaetano pointed out drily. 'So, please let me take you home now and call an end to this charade!'

'It's not a charade…it's my life!' she exclaimed, anxiety flooding her expressive face at the prospect of change being forced on her. 'I don't want to be unreasonable, Gaetano.'

'Then don't be. You give a little, I give a little? That's how people negotiate what works best for them.'

'Is that the former hedge-fund manager talking?' Lara almost whispered. 'The guy who insisted on teaching me algebra?'

His beautiful eyes gleamed with amusement, and he ran his finger along her full bottom lip. 'Admit it. I was an extraordinarily good mansplainer.'

And she snorted with laughter and her face lit up. He bent down because even seated on the desk she was still tiny. His hands found her glorious mass of hair and tangled in it as he drew her closer. He was hard as a rock, pulsing with energy and hunger but he *knew* he shouldn't have his hands on her, shouldn't be that close, only he could not resist the strength of that urge even while he was waiting for her to stop him because, as he had cause to know, Lara was very, *very* efficient at stopping a man in his tracks if she chose to. Only on this occasion she defied his expectations by leaning into him, tilting up her incredibly pretty face, those amazing eyes locked to him. Desire shot through him in an unstoppable surge.

Lara closed her eyes when he kissed her.

She had never ever wanted anything so much, aside of the very first time they had made love. One lean hand framed her face, long fingers stroking her smooth freckled skin, and her heart was pounding so hard that she was vaguely surprised that it didn't burst right out of her chest with sheer excitement. His warm firm mouth tasted hers and she kissed him back with fervour, her hands flying up to smooth over his broad shoulders and then lace into his luxuriant black hair. He groaned into her mouth as her tongue met his and eased her closer, pushing his way between her legs until he gained the actual physical contact that both their bodies seemed to be screaming to experience.

She could feel how aroused Gaetano was through the taut fabric of his trousers and a steamy blur of memory almost consumed her as she clenched down deep inside in the place she hadn't thought about since she had last been with him. Her breasts were tight and swollen, her core hot and damp. She wanted more, had never wanted more so badly but the warning voice that screamed the reminder, 'divorce', in the back of her mind refused to be silenced. Stinging regret made her remove her hands from his hair and press them against his chest instead to separate them.

'We can't do this…' she muttered shakily.

Gaetano pushed an unsteady hand through his messy hair and stepped back from her as if he were stepping back from a seriously deep drop on a cliff edge. He knew she was right, and he said nothing because to his mind there was nothing to say. The same attraction that had first drawn them together still lingered but should *not* be acted on, he reminded himself grimly. He was letting his body and his almost overpowering emotional state of mind lead him down the wrong path. His big brother had programmed him from an early age to step away, step back, always cool off before he acted on any emotion and Dario at his elbow was a little like a mini-Vittorio, always urging Gaetano to be practical, sensible, self-disciplined and controlled. As if he had ever been anything else, his entire life through…with the single exception of those crazy weeks with Lara, he acknowledged guiltily.

'We both got upset and there was a bit of a timeslip there,' Lara mumbled, making excuses for them both when what he really wanted from her was a slap or a kick for his having dared to touch her again. Why? Only punishment would have made him feel less culpable for yet another mistake where she was concerned.

She slid off the desk, her head bent, and scooped up the mop.

'Let me take you home now, draw a line under this,' Gaetano muttered tautly.

Fortunately, that gave her something else to think about and she was grateful for it, so grateful not to have to think of how she had surrendered to his lust the instant she was offered the opportunity. The job?

'You can stay home with Freddy until we get all this sorted out,' Gaetano suggested. 'I'd be very grateful.'

He was saying *please* the only way he knew how. Underneath he was still the man she had married, she registered, just a smoother, slicker version, superbly well groomed and with his phenomenal intensity currently muted. And he wasn't happy. He wasn't happy at all that she had let him kiss her—she could tell by the furrow on his brow, the tightness round his mouth, even the veiled darkness of his gaze. There was no triumph and nothing nasty or threatening about his brooding silence. Unfortunately, Lara didn't want to *be* aware of such things, not with a man she had had to learn to get by without, not with a man who was in the process of divorcing her. She had to stiffen her backbone and be…what was that word? That impossible word he had voiced to her the night before?

Impersonal.

Gaetano lowered his mobile phone as she repacked the cleaning trolley. 'Just leave it here. They're sending another cleaning operative out to finish the job.'

'And why would they do that when I'm letting them down?'

'You're not letting anyone down, Lara,' Gaetano sliced back at her grimly. 'I'm paying them to let you go without a fuss just as I paid the guard to let me into the building. That's how I handle problems in my world, and you may be grimacing right now because you see that as immoral but some day you'll be watching our son do the exact same thing.'

Lara reddened that he had read her so accurately and then paled at the thought of her precious Freddy growing into the same kind of man. 'I don't approve,' she admitted stiffly.

'You don't need to approve. It is expected that people of my status pay for their privilege and that if others go that extra mile for our benefit, we reward them. That's my life and it has *always* been that way. Billionaires don't generally get handed something for nothing,' he said gently, borrowing one of the phrases she had once taught him, a phrase her grandmother had taught her.

With that final explanation, he stooped and grasped the hem of the overall she wore to whip it over her head and scrunch it into a ball that he tossed into a waste basket as they waited for the lift. The beanie had already gone missing. Lara was too shocked by what he had just said to react.

'Billionaires? You? Your family?' Lara croaked, shocked almost to silence by that concept, that reminder that they came from totally different worlds. 'You're *that* rich? Seriously?'

A smile broke out on Gaetano's lean darkly handsome face. He didn't bother mentioning that he didn't have a family aside of her and the son he had yet to meet. He simply savoured the shock on her startled face and wished Dario had had the opportunity to both see and hear that little snatch of dialogue. But then, possibly, Dario would never understand that the kind of woman he had married didn't have a mercenary bone in her body. Just like him she had flaws, but that was not one of them.

'I wrecked your hair.' Lara sighed, standing on tiptoe to brush it out of his eyes and smooth it down again and then stilling in mortification at that act of overfamiliarity. 'Sorry, I think I'm too tired to be doing this with you…'

'We'll go and get a bite to eat,' Gaetano announced, urging her into the lift.

'No, let's keep things a little more…detached,' she selected, striving to employ the vocabulary he had used on her. 'I have Alice's car parked outside, so I don't need a lift, and then you can come and see Freddy tomorrow when he's awake.'

It was sensible advice, but Gaetano discovered that he didn't want to hear it. He frowned. 'We have to talk some time.'

'But it doesn't have to be right now this very minute,' she stated calmly, recognising his innate impatience from the past. The more time she spent with Gaetano, the more she caught glimpses of the guy she had married, and she couldn't afford to encourage that painful sense of connection that was now so out of place in their broken relationship.

Alice was in the hall waiting for her the moment she put her key in the front door. 'Are you on your own?' she asked, peering over the top of her diminutive friend and all around her. 'Gaetano is *so* gorgeous, Lara. Not at all surprised that you fell for him like a ton of bricks! I couldn't believe my eyes when he said who he was.'

'He was here?' Lara queried in dismay.

'Yes, looking for you and Freddy. He said he'd forgotten that you worked in the evenings.'

Lara flushed and avoided her friend's gaze. 'He came to see me at work. He's going to visit tomorrow to meet Freddy.'

'That sounds like a keen parent-to-be, at least,' Alice quipped, switching on the kettle as Lara followed her through to the kitchen. 'But I'll be frank... I saw him getting into a limousine out there. Clearly, he's wealthier than the average baby daddy.'

'Yes, Gaetano's not average in any way,' Lara conceded awkwardly, still reluctant to share the entire truth with her friend, especially after Gaetano had referred to his desire for discretion. She loved Alice to death but was painfully conscious that she would talk her head off to everyone she knew if she learned that Gaetano was a royal.

'He's definitely going to pay support for Freddy,' she told the brunette, willing to share other information. 'He asked me to quit my job and stay home with him and, to be honest, while he's this young I would enjoy that. I can't say being a cleaner is so much fun that I will stick with it if I don't have to.'

'And you could study while you're at home, start catching up again,' Alice commented with enthusiasm. 'I still think it's so unfair that your mother was so thoughtless about your education.'

For thoughtless, read selfish, Lara ruminated wryly. Every time her mother, Eliza, had broken up with a boyfriend, she had moved to another city and Lara had been pulled out of school to be changed to another one. Once they had moved abroad, Eliza had pretty much stopped worrying altogether about her daughter receiving an education. After all, Lara had been more useful to her helping out at home or working in a bar kitchen or waitressing.

Alice gave her a warm smile. 'I'm so happy that Gaetano is willing to give you support without making a fight out of it like some men do.'

'No, he's not likely to be difficult in that line.' Lara drained her cup and put it in the dishwasher. 'I'm going to go to bed early. I'm very tired and I want to be fresh for tomorrow.'

She hovered over Freddy's cot. He was fast asleep, stretched out like a little starfish, as good as his father had once been at hogging all the available mattress space. As soon as she thought that she tried to squash such thoughts because looking back in time did her no favours. What was gone was *gone*.

But by the time she was climbing into bed, the weight of memories had grown too heavy to avoid and just as quickly she slid back into that very first week spent with Gaetano.

Right from the start there had been a curious synchronicity between them, an ease as if they had known each other for years. It had probably been the hothouse effect of it being just the two of them in an isolated snowbound house, she reflected now. The day after the first night she had climbed up the hill and found his rucksack, dragging it back to the house and presenting it to him as if she had won the lottery, somehow expecting his every question to be magically answered by what they found within. They had discovered only a passport and an extraordinary amount of cash concealed in a hidden security pocket.

His passport had told them that his name was Gaetano di Santis and he was British, and was twenty-seven years old. It had not occurred to either of them that he might have dual nationality or that the reason he was travelling on his British passport was probably that he had sought that anonymity. The day after that they had gone up the hill together to search for a mobile phone, convinced he must have had one and had lost it as well, but they hadn't found one.

Her friend, Cathy, and her husband had given permission by text for Gaetano to stay on in the house with her. His condition would have condemned him to a homeless shelter but the cash he had would have got him a hotel room. She had cringed at the prospect of Gaetano spending Christmas alone someplace else. And in between Lara teaching him the rudiments of basic cookery and how to chop firewood, Gaetano had taught her algebra and how to play chess. He was a keen reader and, fortunately, Cathy's shelves had been packed with books.

The snow had been gone within days and Dr Beresford had called in, calming Gaetano's concerns and telling him that temporary amnesia was much more common than he might think after a head injury and that it was even possible that some stress in his life prior to the accident could have inhibited his memory to protect him and allow him time to recover his equilibrium.

'The mind is a wonderful thing,' the elderly woman had told him cheerfully. 'Most people with amnesia recover their memory within weeks or months but I must warn you that it doesn't always work that way and that perhaps you should consult a professional in the field.'

Gaetano, however, had baulked at the suggestion that he confide in anyone else, making Lara realise that he was much more reserved than most people she knew. They had been together day after day, and she had taken him everywhere with her. She had taken him to church, introduced him to the local priest and he had discovered with relief that the rituals of worship were familiar to him. She had taken him shopping when he wanted new clothes, amused by his fastidiousness, his awareness of fashion, so unlike the men she was accustomed to meeting. They had gone to the supermarket together, the post office and even the pub, where he'd decided that he didn't like beer very much.

Their relationship had moved at breakneck speed. On the tenth day he had told her that he was falling in love with her, and she had been shattered that a man could be that open and honest with her. That was when she had fully opened her heart to Gaetano to admit that she felt the same. That was also when the barriers had come down and she had stopped saying no when it came to more than a little light petting because of course they had become incredibly close spending so much time as a couple. He was also the first guy she had been with who didn't pressure her for sex and who took no for an answer without making her feel bad about it.

In every sense of the word, it had been a love affair and that constant closeness, sharing and talking, had accelerated the process.

Gaetano's passionate nature had made everything run faster than the speed of light.

'I want you. I know I shouldn't say it when I can't prove it for a fact, but I don't believe I could *ever* have wanted a woman as much as I want you, *bambola*.'

And that was it, her defences had crumbled. That same night he had also asked her to marry him.

'I'll never be as sure of anything as I am of my feelings for you,' Gaetano had sworn. 'I want to know you're mine in every way and that means I put a ring on your finger and my own and we do it legally.'

She had said yes straight away, not a single doubt in her head either, and the next day they had gone to see the priest to see if they could get married in time for Christmas. Only Dr Beresford had sounded a note of caution, pointing out that Gaetano still knew next to nothing about himself but, like young lovers everywhere, neither of them had listened because neither of them had had the smallest desire to play it safe. They had wanted to plunge on in their lives and savour every moment to the fullest…

CHAPTER FIVE

THE NEXT DAY, Lara was up at the crack of dawn, tidying the house, making sure everything was presentable, at least, for a man who had grown up in a palace. Thinking that made her roll her eyes and grimace at her own thoughts.

She had nothing in common with Gaetano, absolutely nothing, she told herself firmly. They had been ships that passed, people who, under normal circumstances, would never have met each other. They had had a fling, a foolish fling, that was *all*, she programmed herself. He was *not* the love of her life as she had once fondly believed. In fact, were it not for her son, Gaetano would be the worst mistake she had ever made because *nobody* had ever made her feel as miserably wretched and unhappy as he had.

Sadly, two years earlier, rejection from her

nearest and dearest had not been a new experience for Lara. At the age of nine she had gone from being a much-loved daddy's girl to being an often irritating burden and unwelcome expense to her surviving parent. That had been tough. Her grandparents had done much the same thing to her. They had warned her from the outset that when she reached eighteen, they expected her to move out and make her own life. She was grateful they had given her a home when she was desperate for one at sixteen but pretty hurt that, in spite of her warmth towards them, they had never viewed her as more than a nod of respect towards the memory of the adored son who had died after adopting Lara.

Gaetano texted her a time for his arrival. She dressed Freddy in jeans and a sweater, dampened down his riot of black curls and fed him well to keep him in a good mood.

Gaetano asked her if he could pick them up on the road at the rear of the house. Lara winced because she had assumed that Gaetano would see Freddy at their home, but she couldn't come up quickly enough with an argument to protest the idea of them travelling elsewhere. Perhaps he was thinking of them going to the park, she reckoned with more enthusiasm because Freddy was easier handled outdoors. Putting on coats and tucking her son into his pushchair, she hurried out of the front door to walk round the corner, wondering if this was the kind of 'discreet' that Gaetano had alluded to while looking down an almost empty suburban road and thinking it was a decided overreaction.

A huge limousine idled by the kerb, nothing discreet about that in such a neighbourhood, she reckoned with wry amusement, lifting Freddy out and beginning to collapse the pushchair before the driver and another man intervened, seemingly shocked that she would think to do such a thing for herself. The passenger door was opened. Gaetano was not inside. So, not the park, then. She settled Freddy into the plush car seat already awaiting him and did up the straps.

The car took them straight back to the Victorian mansion and Lara winced, feeling underdressed in her worn jeans, sweatshirt and padded jacket. It was a relief when Gaetano greeted her alone in the hall, nobody to question her about who she was, nobody to judge her appearance with scorn. And her attention was immediately taken by Gaetano, sheathed in jeans and a shirt, looking very much as he had two years earlier.

When Lara walked in, Gaetano's fists clenched. He was on edge because so much was riding on this meeting. And then Lara blew in, fresh as a daisy with her strawberry blonde waves floating back from her face like in some slow-motion scene in a romantic movie, and he was rivetted to the spot, noting the freckles scattered across her nose. Exactly six, he *remembered* that. And those eyes, set below arched brows, the purest breathtaking aquamarine above her soft pink lips. There was nothing honourable about his plan, indeed it was ruthless, although not quite as ruthless as his friend Dario's would have been. And Dario's plan, while strictly necessary in such a dangerous situation, would be cruel and it would frighten her. Whatever Lara might expect from him, she did not deserve any form of a scare.

A tiny noise escaped the large wriggling bundle in her arms, and she set it down and for the first time Gaetano registered that the bundle was actually *his* son and definitely what he should have focused his entire interest on, rather than on his son's mother. Lara knelt down to remove Freddy's coat and the little boy slowly turned round, taking in his unfamiliar surroundings with interest.

Gaetano got down on his level to meet him, but Freddy was already past him, moving at toddler speed, having espied the enormous flower arrangement seated on a low table to the rear of the hall.

Aghast, Lara plunged forward as her son reached up a grasping hand, and she shouted, 'Freddy, *no*!'

Freddy looked back at her with huge chocolate-button eyes, a flush on his cheeks of rage at her rebuke. Before she could even reach him, he had flung himself down in a passion to kick and scream and sob.

Mortification claiming her, Lara stilled beside Gaetano and said in a stifled voice, 'This is Freddy. It's best not to lift him until he gets the worst over with because that only makes him fight and shout louder.'

Involuntarily, Gaetano was fascinated. 'My brother once showed me a photo of me doing the exact same thing,' he told her, disconcerting her when she had expected an admonishment from him and at least a hint of criticism that she might not be the best parent in a disciplinary sense.

'What age were you?'

'About two. It was to teach me what I was capable of when I lost my temper.'

'No wonder you hate getting angry. I think that was brutal,' Lara opined. 'As Freddy learns more words, he will hopefully grow out of the meltdowns. Right now, it's his only way of expressing his frustration.'

While they had been talking and ignoring him, Freddy had sat up, his tear-streaked little face now intent on Gaetano, who was unfamiliar to him.

'*Madonna mia*…he is the picture of me as a child,' Gaetano almost whispered. 'Except for the curls.'

'I don't know where the curls came from. Looks wise he didn't get much of me, either,' Lara framed as Freddy toddled over to Gaetano and grabbed his knees to look up at him. 'As you can see, he's very friendly and outgoing.'

Gaetano startled her by bending down and scooping their son up into his arms with every appearance of enthusiasm. 'Let's go upstairs. This house has a playroom and I brought in more toys and…er, a nanny,' he completed rather stiffly.

'What on earth would you need a nanny for when I'm here?'

'I was thinking of a future visit, when perhaps you might want to leave him,' Gaetano lied, shading that story a second later by adding more convincingly. 'And, of course, if we're going to talk, that wouldn't be easy with a young child around.'

'Good grief…a nanny? How long are you planning to stay here?' Lara asked in astonishment, watching his lean darkly handsome face tense until her attention fell on the huge and fabulous portrait above the landing. 'That is gorgeous,' she whispered, in awe of the beautiful brunette and the fabulous blue ball gown and jewellery she sported. 'I wonder who she was.'

'My mother,' Gaetano informed her, his tone clipped. 'When he died, my grandfather left this entire estate to me. He had cut off communication with her long before she died. It was a generous legacy but I wish he'd given me the chance to get to know him instead.'

'You never met the man?'

'No. My mother was an only child and she

disappointed him, much like she disappointed me. Possibly he feared that I would do something similar, so he never sought me out.'

Lara swallowed hard, aware that she was discussing a sensitive topic because she had done her homework on Gaetano's background as far as was possible with only the Internet as a research tool. 'She left you when you were very young,' she remarked ruefully.

'Walked out on my father and me, divorced him and, only weeks later, married a Swiss billionaire who lived in Brazil,' Gaetano completed unemotionally.

'Did she ever have any more child—?'

'No. I think we can take it as a given that she wasn't the motherly type,' he incised very drily. 'She died three years ago, I believe. Her husband informed me after she had passed, although I can't think why because I have no memory of her whatsoever.'

Lara recognised the coolness of his gaze shielding his enduring pain over that hurtful truth and her heart went out to him because she knew how such a wound lingered in the mind. 'Perhaps the same could be said for my birth mother—I mean, her not being the motherly type. Remember I was adopted,' she reminded him.

'Yes, I recall that. What do you know about your birth parents?'

'Nothing whatsoever. I decided not to look into it—'

'Why not?'

Lara flushed. Two years earlier, she hadn't shared much beyond the barest facts of her life with Gaetano because she had been ashamed of how unprepossessing even her adoptive background was. 'I just wasn't interested,' she said uncomfortably. 'Getting curious could be a mistake, too. I could be a child born after some awful event like rape... who knows?'

'You're too pessimistic. That's not like you,' Gaetano pronounced with a frown as he pushed open a door into an old-fashioned children's nursery. 'You once impressed me as an incurable optimist.'

'Yes...well, we all put our best face on when we think we're falling in love,' Lara countered, lifting her chin.

'Think?' Gaetano echoed with emphasis as he lowered Freddy and their son sped to-

wards the box of brightly coloured toys he had glimpsed.

'Yes,' Lara confirmed with determination. 'I don't think it was real for either of us. You needed something or someone to ground you when you had no memory.'

'Oh, don't stop there,' Gaetano urged sardonically, getting down on the rug beside Freddy to show him how to open the big red bus he was investigating. Of course, she was telling the truth, he acknowledged inwardly and, since he had reached the same conclusion on his own, why exactly was he arguing the point? Or had he only reached that conclusion because it was a coping mechanism to persuade himself that what he had grieved at losing had never been real in the first place?

'What do you think you were feeling if it wasn't love?'

Lara compressed her lips while her cheeks burned. 'I was very attracted to you, and I hadn't felt like that before.'

'Lust, then. How edifying to discover that now about the woman I married.'

Lara wanted to throw something at him. Saving face around Gaetano was an uphill challenge. She could feel the heat in her cheeks as though she were boiling alive because lying didn't come naturally to her. But forcing herself into that mindset, even when she didn't believe it, had been a necessary part of her recovery process. Shoving a smile on her face as she told herself that she could afford to be the bigger person now that she had got over him, she removed her coat and got down on the rug on the other side of her son. 'I was very attached to you,' she admitted grudgingly.

Somewhat mollified by that admission, Gaetano was already questioning why he cared and why conversations with Lara went in directions that they never ever went with anyone else. And as the answer dawned on him, his taut expression vanished, and he smiled brilliantly at her. 'You're the only person I know who treats me normally.'

'What's that supposed to mean?'

'The job title gets in the way of normality. Nobody but Dario ever tells me anything that I don't want to hear, which is why I value him so highly. I appreciate that you have a different attitude from him.'

'The first time we met he looked at me as though I had *conned* you into marrying me.'

'He's inclined to be too protective towards me but then, basically, protecting me legally is his career. Dario and I went to the same English boarding school but even he doesn't speak to me the way you do. Probably because he's from Mosvakia and even he can never quite forget who I am.'

'I'm sorry I'm so…blunt.' She used the word awkwardly, feeling embarrassed that she just had no idea how to treat royalty even though she was still married to the man. Freddy chose that moment to crawl into her lap, curl up and close his eyes with a sleepy sigh.

As he watched that display of his son's trust and dependency on his mother, a shimmering smile chased the tension from Gaetano's darkly handsome face and his eyes glittered pure gold below his curling black lashes. Lara's heart skipped a beat and fireworks flared in her stomach as she looked at him. He could light her up like a fire inside herself just with a certain look. And, uneasily aware that she should no longer be reacting that way to Gaetano, Lara scrambled upright slowly because Freddy was quite a weight and said, 'Is there any place I can put him down for a nap?'

'He's that tired *already*?' Gaetano asked in surprise.

'He's been on the go since six-thirty and I usually let him have an hour to nap about now.'

'It's fortunate that I had a new cot delivered. The original was an antique,' Gaetano told her with a chuckle as he vaulted upright and reached out quite naturally to ease his son out of her arms. 'You forget that he's still a baby. He looks older as I did because he's going to be tall.'

He walked over to the cot she hadn't noticed in the corner, and she censured herself for being so wrapped up in Gaetano's presence that she was almost blind to her surroundings. He laid the little boy down on top of the mattress and she leant over to slip off his shoes. 'It's warm here so I won't cover him, but I'll just nip downstairs and collect his bunny in case he wakes up.'

Before Gaetano could intervene, she had flashed out of the room and he stood on the landing, watching her speed downstairs to gather up the bag she had brought with her and return. Breathless, she tucked a shabby bunny into the cot beside their son, brushed his hair back from his face and smiled tenderly down at her child. 'He sleeps like a log. Nothing short of an earthquake would wake him when he's tired.'

And just like that, Gaetano knew he would be doing the right thing, even if most other people, including Dario, would think that what he was about to do was the very worst thing he could do. She was a wonderful mother and, for all their sakes, he would not part her from her son, no, not even for a day. He was praying that she was *still* that naïve woman he had married.

'You said something about us talking…' Lara reminded him.

Gaetano shifted position with the strangest hint of hesitancy. Even without his memory Gaetano had been a very decisive guy. 'I have something very important to say to you,' he announced, burnished dark eyes suddenly homing in on her wide gaze and holding it fast. 'Let's move across the corridor. It's my private suite and we won't be disturbed by the staff there.'

As he pressed a bellpush in the wall, she frowned, everything knocked out of kilter by his statement as she tried to fathom out what he could possibly want to say.

'The nanny knows to come and take care of our son when I ring the bell,' he explained.

'I didn't know big houses still had systems like that in operation,' she confided.

'It's a convenience in a building this size,' Gaetano pointed out pragmatically as he ushered her through a door opposite into a gracious drawing room.

Lara walked over to one of the three windows, which were grandly draped in extravagant curtains. She gazed out at the rolling lawn with its woodland groves and the park beyond where she thought she could see a herd of deer grazing. Gaetano lived in another world and the surroundings inside and out were a distinctly painful reminder.

'I suggest that we forget the divorce idea for the present...'

Lara's eyes rounded and she spun back to him, her throat tightening with nerves and that awful sense of having lost her way in the conversation because she could not think of a single reason why he should propose such an idea. 'Right…' she muttered uncertainly, waiting for him to finish talking, which he seemed to be in no hurry to do.

His high cheekbones were flushed, his dark eyes very level and intent on her, *so* intent that she went rigid with self-consciousness, her small frame bracing as though she were under attack.

'I would like for us to try a reconciliation instead.'

Lara was so shocked and so utterly unprepared for that suggestion that she lost all her colour, her small face turning wan. *'Really?'* she mumbled weakly.

Gaetano didn't feel that her turning as white as a ghost was much encouragement and, that fast, he was wondering if there was another man in her life. He stalked forward, angry destructive feelings tugging at him even as he rammed them back down again, determined to stay in control because so much hung on her answer.

'I don't know what to say. You've really taken me by surprise,' Lara confided, turning away and then turning back, not wishing to be rude when he had had the courage to make such a proposal.

Gaetano halted mere inches from her, making her extraordinarily conscious of his height and forcing her to turn her face up to look at him. It was a comfort to acknowledge that Gaetano looked every bit as tense as she felt and deadly serious.

'Hear me out at least,' he asked her in a taut undertone. 'I want us to be a family. I didn't have that and neither did you, from what little you have told me. Freddy deserves parents willing to make the effort to be together. But to be frank, I also want *you* back, not just Freddy…'

Lara was so shattered by that assurance that her knees went all wobbly. She blinked rapidly, her heartbeat thundering inside her tight chest, making ordinary breathing a challenge. *I want you back.* Never ever had she even dreamt of hearing such a declaration from Gaetano. She had left everything she felt for him behind her…hadn't she? Wasn't that, for her own sake, all old history not to be revisited under any circumstances?

'And, to be even more frank, I haven't had a single happy moment since you left me,' Gaetano framed in an almost disjointed rush.

'I do the job I'm expected to do and the job is my entire life, which is far from ideal.'

Her soft heart clenched. Why had she always assumed that he would be delighted to take the throne and become King? Not a single *happy* moment? A rush of tears stung the backs of her eyes and she glanced down at the rug beneath their feet, the colours blurring as she struggled to control her emotions, but just then she was feeling more emotions than she could possibly handle all at once. Disbelief, bewilderment, a literal terror of making another mistake but, ultimately, a sense of pure joy. The very first thought that raced through her, shaming her, making her despise herself was that she *wanted* him, wanted him back yesterday for that matter, had probably never stopped wanting him back since she'd first walked away from him.

'I couldn't be a queen,' she declared with pained certainty. 'I haven't got what it would take to be *that*.'

'You don't have to be a queen anywhere but behind closed doors in our private apartments. I'm not expecting you to do anything in public unless you decide that you want to do so…which eventually you might do when you realise that the job's not quite as intimidating as it seems,' he assured her smoothly. 'But here, now at the *beginning*, I would expect nothing from you beyond being my wife and Freddy's mother.'

'OK,' she said hoarsely, that assent falling from her lips before she could even think better of it. 'Let's go for it…we can only try, there's nothing wrong with trying.'

And she stood there in a total daze of incredulity but deciding really *was* that simple, that fast, because for two long years she had been kidding herself that she had got over him and it had all been a lie to save face. She had thought that he had rejected her but now it seemed as though she must have got that wrong. Only, what if they got together again and their marriage fell apart for a second time? It happened, didn't it? People found that good intentions were insufficient to keep a relationship afloat.

Even so, wouldn't trying to be a couple again be the braver option? At least giving both of them a chance to prove that they could be together? What if Gaetano changed his mind again? What if she got hurt again?

But why was she even thinking such thoughts when he had voiced words that might have described her own feelings?

Not a single happy moment…

CHAPTER SIX

A SENSE OF intense relief ran through Gaetano and crashed over him like a wave: he had got Lara back. He could do it; he could fake *anything* for the sake of the three of them!

And even though he had decidedly fudged the truth, he had not told any direct lies, he reasoned, determined as he was not to see himself as a deceiver or a liar. He would do everything within his power to make her happy and he would offer her every possible support. Above all, the best feature of Lara was that what you saw was what you got. She had none of the unscrupulous personality twists that even *he* rejoiced in. In addition, she had a very small ego in comparison to most people he met. She couldn't lie to save her life and she trusted him. In every way he would prove worthy of that trust, he reassured himself.

While Gaetano was engaged in intense self-examination, Lara was in a dizzy whirl of happiness. Gaetano had *missed* her. He had looked back and accepted how *good* they were together, had evidently only seen that value when it was too late to keep her by his side. In the spirit of newly rediscovered confidence, reminiscent of the Lara she had been with Gaetano two years earlier before his changed attitude had stripped her of such assurance, Lara closed the distance between them and stretched up to wind two slender arms round his neck.

Momentarily, Gaetano was stunned by that forward move on her part but just as quickly, his body reacting with instant visceral hunger, he was on board with the invitation. He stared down at her with scorching dark golden eyes and covered her mouth with his in a breathtakingly urgent kiss. His desire was that immediate, that driven by need. Lara gasped under that onslaught of passion, feeling the instinctive response of her body to his just as she had on that office desk the day before. But now, everything was different, she thought fondly, slender fingers stretching up into his luxuriant hair with that wicked, wanton possessiveness it had taken so long for her to shed after leaving him. She wasn't about to think about the other women he would have been with since, she *wasn't*! New book, clean page, she urged herself.

Without hesitation, Gaetano bent down and swept her up fully into his arms and her slip-on shoes fell off.

As he lifted his mouth from hers to thrust open a door, Lara giggled. 'So, I'm getting the full *Gone with the Wind* experience, am I?'

'No,' Gaetano retorted with a sudden slanting grin of amused appreciation that few Mosvakians would have realised their serious king was even capable of. 'The very last thing I'm about to say right now is, *Frankly, I don't give a damn*—'

'I didn't even realise you were a movie buff…you didn't recognise *Dr Zhivago* when we first met.'

'I'm not but my former sister-in-law, Giulia, is, and as a teenager I watched her favourites with her many times.'

'*Former?* Don't you count her as family any more now that she's a widow?' Lara queried.

'She's remarried and living in Italy now.

I'm happy that she's found love with someone new. Her union with my brother was more a marriage of convenience.'

'Oh.' As Gaetano had laid her down on a big bed and was in the process of stripping her with an indecent haste that was insanely seductive, Lara's ability to make rational comments was on the retreat.

Her boots, socks and jeans were gone in a moment, and she sat up to remove her own sweatshirt, marvelling at how her whole world had changed focus since her arrival at the mansion. 'This...*us*, doesn't quite feel real yet.'

Gaetano stared at her sitting there in an unmatched bra and pants of the most ordinary kind of white unadorned lingerie. She was slender and yet just curvy enough in all the right places. Her skin gleamed like a pearl in moonlight while her beautiful hair glowed like the dawn in the wintry shadows of the bedroom. She had the most extraordinary effect on the way he thought, he acknowledged absently, lost in sensual appreciation.

'You look incredibly sexy,' he murmured hoarsely, one hand reaching round his back to haul off the casual shirt he had teamed with designer jeans.

In many ways, the mysterious workings of Gaetano's mind had always been a closed book to Lara. She could see nothing sexy in herself, only flaws like her skinny legs and the faint stretchmarks on her stomach. She glanced down uncomfortably at her service-able bra and knickers and marvelled that a man of his experience and wealth could still find her so desirable. And she knew that he wasn't saying it for effect when that admira-tion was openly etched onto his lean darkly handsome face. Yet it was he, Gaetano di San-tis, who totally took *her* breath away, poised there, his chest bare, smooth dark olive-tinted shoulders, washboard delineated abs and lean hips on display. He was gorgeous. She was *not*. Even before she'd discovered that he was royalty there had, for her, always been a credibility gap attached to their love and marriage. She had struggled to believe that he could genuinely love her as much as she loved him. With a dexterous wriggle she slid beneath the duvet, hiding her imperfect self.

He peeled off his jeans and boxers with the same careless speed, pushing back the bedding to reach for her. 'I can barely believe that I'm with you again.'

'You're not the only one,' she whispered before his mouth found hers again and that wild, seething sense of excitement started to climb inside her like an unquenchable flame.

Gaetano still wanted her more than any other woman. That was a miraculous fact to Lara and the knowledge strengthened her. She ran her hands down over his chest, loving the feel of the smooth brown skin and the curling black hair smattering the centre of his broad chest.

'Don't stop,' Gaetano groaned, throwing his dark head back on the pillows and resting back like a very willing sacrifice.

She found him with her roaming fingers, already long and thick and pulsing with desire. She shimmied down the bed, the tip of her tongue tracing her path, and his fingers laced tautly into her hair. It was as if some magical clock had turned back time. As she traced that velvety smooth tip, his hips angled up to her and a hoarse sound of pleasure was wrenched from him.

So she was surprised when he stopped her, hauling her back up to him to kiss her with ferocious hunger, rolling her over and tugging off her remaining garments with scant ceremony. 'I'm not likely to last very long,' he warned her gruffly.

'I'll survive,' Lara muttered, amazed that he should worry about something she considered unimportant. She didn't need or expect perfect after so much time had passed, she simply longed for that irreplaceable physical closeness to be renewed.

With his lips he traced the pointed buds of her nipples and a wave of sensitised reaction rippled through her, lighting up the warmth blossoming between her legs. She couldn't stay still as he traced the damp swollen folds there with one skilled hand and used the other to make her quiver and whimper as he sucked hard on the pouting peaks of her breasts.

'What is it about you?' he muttered in a roughened undertone. 'You turn me on faster than anyone else ever did.'

'Stop talking,' she framed shakily, parting her thighs round his lean hips, tugging her knees back to encourage him. 'I can't wait.'

'I'm trying to take this slow, *bambola*,' Gaetano reproved thickly.

Lara uttered a breathy little cry of impatience and shifted against him, quite deliberately sliding her heated core over his jutting erection.

Gaetano bit out a groan and gripped her slender hips to raise her to him. Mere seconds later, he was exactly where she wanted him to be, reintroducing her to sensations she had almost forgotten. The stretching fullness of his invasion, the glorious friction of his retreat and advance. Wound round him like a vine, she moaned in delight, hands skating down his long smooth back in appreciation as she angled up to him for more. With a ragged sound fleeing his parted lips he stared down at her with joy, speeding up, finally pounding into her welcoming body until what she hadn't believed was that important happened anyway, grabbing her up in a great storm of corporeal sensation. The world behind her lowered eyelids flashed white and her slender frame arched for a timeless moment before fireworks flared inside her and she went incandescent, her whole body flooding with blissful pleasure.

With Lara still wrapped round him, Gaetano released a sigh of immense relaxation and snaked out a hand to lift his phone.

She listened to him ordering champagne and raised her brows.

'Champagne and strawberries?' she whispered. 'Are we still pretending we're on a movie set?'

'No, we're celebrating. I've got my very hot wife back in my bed,' he told her smoothly, flashing her a triumphant grin. 'Mission accomplished.'

'I suppose I could raise a glass to my even hotter husband,' Lara murmured, clashing with glittering dark eyes that left her breathless.

It was an effort to get out of bed after the champagne and strawberries and she felt more than a little giggly in the aftermath. Only her concern for Freddy and what he might be having for lunch, nanny or not, roused her from the bed, in spite of Gaetano's attempt to keep her there. She felt happy, incredibly, extravagantly happy, and feeling like that after spending so long just bumping along the bottom of life while being a working mother also felt strange. And she almost felt guilty. Why guilt? she questioned herself as she stepped out of the shower that Gaetano had just vacated. Didn't she feel that she deserved to be happy? Or was she just afraid that somehow something or somebody would steal that happiness away from her again?

As she emerged from the bathroom, fully clothed and rather flushed and unsure of herself in the aftermath of the life-changing decision she had reached at the speed of light, she heard male voices, one of them Gaetano's, in the next room because the bedroom door wasn't fully closed. Breathing in deep, she returned to the sitting room to retrieve her shoes. The first thing she noticed was that Gaetano's companion was Dario and he dealt her a shaken look before glancing away, swiftly wiping all expression from his bearded face. Lara reddened because it was very obvious that she and Gaetano must have shared a bed again but, on another level, she was pleased by Dario's astonishment. Close friend Dario might be but, plainly, Gaetano had not confided in his lawyer before asking his estranged wife to reconcile with him. It was a relief to know that there were limits to that friendship.

'I'm just going to check on Freddy,' Lara murmured, ducking past both men, who appeared to be locked into some sort of serious discussion. 'And then I'll need to see about picking up Iris from school... Iris, my friend Alice's little girl.'

'No, you had better hear this first,' Gaetano countered with compressed lips. 'I'm afraid the press have got the jump on us and are presently besieging the house where you live.'

Lara looked at him in horror. 'Oh, my word...'

'If you give me your keys, my security team will remove your belongings and my son's to bring them here.'

'I can't just walk out of my whole life like that,' Lara began shakily, her eyes huge in her pale face. 'Alice depends on me for childcare, for goodness' sake. I can't leave my best friend in the lurch—'

'It's not a problem, *bambola mia*,' Gaetano cut in smoothly. 'Alice and Iris should come here for tonight at least until the press have given up. They'll be perfectly comfortable here and we have a nanny who is capable of taking on any childcare concerns you may have. *Relax*.'

Inadvertently, Lara glanced at Dario, somewhat comforted by the reality that he had only travelled from shocked to seemingly stunned into silence while Gaetano outlined his solution to their predicament.

Gaetano glanced at Dario. 'Have an announcement of our marriage and Freddy's birth released at home and then here in the UK. What is his birthdate?'

Lara told him and Dario dug out a notebook and made a note of it.

'We no longer have to be discreet,' Gaetano informed his employee.

'Yes, sir. Is there anything else I can do for you?' the other man enquired stiffly, his formality pronounced.

'Lara, give Dario your keys and he will pass them on.'

'I'll go with them.'

'To be engulfed by a scrum of paparazzi when you've never faced that challenge before?' Gaetano prompted drily. 'I don't think that's a good idea.'

'I'll phone Alice, ask her to go home and oversee the removal of our stuff if she can.' Lara crossed the corridor into the nursery where Freddy was sitting at a little table cheerfully eating a lunch of finger foods while the nanny, a youthful smiling brunette, supervised him.

'Prince Freddy is very sociable.' Standing up, the young woman approached her and extended her hand politely. 'I'm Ellie Ross. I'm sorry, I don't know who you are—'

'I'm Freddy's mother, Lara,' Lara admitted in a stifled undertone after hearing her son labelled in such a manner as she dug into the bag she had abandoned to find her phone.

She moved back into the sitting room where Gaetano was now sitting at a desk with Dario still hovering. '*Is* Freddy a prince?'

'Crown Prince and my heir,' Gaetano confirmed succinctly. 'Isn't it obvious?'

'No, not when I believed our marriage might not be legal and I thought that for the whole of the two years we were apart,' Lara told him quietly. 'And I don't know anything about royalty except that here in the UK the family have a lot of rules to follow.'

'Mosvakia is not a large country and it's rather more laid-back,' Gaetano responded in a tone of apology. 'Sorry I was short with you. I was miles away, reading something.'

'You are also, automatically as the King's wife, our Queen, Your Majesty,' Dario slotted in.

Lara nodded and nodded again and backed away as though she had been threatened by a hot poker. A queen. *Her*, a queen? A woman who had washed dishes and floors and served in run-down bars as a waitress? A woman who had only three pairs of shoes to her name?

'You shouldn't have said that,' she heard Gaetano reprove before she could close the door again. 'Lara's not some social climber, keen to acquire a title. All that nonsense scares her off!'

Unexpectedly, that little overheard snippet, which told her just how well Gaetano understood her more reticent nature, made Lara straighten her spine, square her slender shoulders and smile. Gaetano had explained her for Dario's benefit, taken her side, shown his support. She brought her phone in the corridor and rang Alice.

'A *king*?' Alice almost shrieked when she was told. 'Are you kidding me? Is this an April Fool or something?'

'Of course I can leave early…joys of being my own boss,' Alice quipped a few minutes later. 'Don't worry. I'll pick up Iris—no need to involve some nanny. Oh, Lara, isn't Freddy just going to *love* being a prince and the centre of attention?'

'Without a doubt,' Lara agreed ruefully.

'I can't wait to talk to you,' her friend admitted. 'When I left the house this morning, you were meeting Gaetano to discuss a divorce and now, only a few hours later…my goodness, that guy moves at supersonic speed!'

'I don't know how I could explain it or explain why I didn't tell you.'

'I'm a complete blabbermouth,' Alice filled in chirpily. 'Always have been, always will be. No explanation required. As for why you're reconciling. Well, no surprise there on your side of the fence.'

'Am I really that predictable?'

'Where he's concerned? I'm afraid so. Look, I'd better run if you've already handed over the keys and you don't want your vast wardrobe stuffed disrespectfully into bin bags,' Alice teased, because they both knew that Lara owned very little. 'See you later.'

Lara joined Freddy in the nursery. Gaetano joined them for Freddy's bath, dive-bombing little boats and ducks with an aeroplane while Freddy screamed with excitement. After a quick supper, her son was ready only for his cot.

'Your friend has arrived and will be joining us for dinner,' Gaetano informed her. 'I gather you hadn't told her who I was.'

'Why would I?' Lara parried ruefully. 'I was Cinderella, but I didn't get my prince.'

Gaetano's eyes flared fiery gold. 'I married you! What greater faith in you and what we had could I have demonstrated?' he demanded in a raw undertone of condemnation that told her she had touched a nerve. 'But you were too weak to seize the moment and you ran away!'

Slowly, Lara straightened. 'That's not how it happened. I wasn't weak and I didn't run away. It's interesting how reality gets massaged and twisted out of shape when people are apart. People develop their own story.'

But once again, Lara was being reminded of what a risk she was taking in trusting Gaetano again. Their unsuccessful past together still hung over them like a dark cloud and could still catapult them into conflict. She could get hurt again, badly hurt, if their marriage failed a second time and that still filled her with fear and insecurity.

Gaetano flexed long brown fingers that had briefly clenched with the force of his emotions and breathed in slow and deep, calming himself down as he recognised the tripwire that had almost entrapped him and damaged what he had gained. 'No doubt we'll talk about it some day but *not* any day soon,' he murmured with smooth emphasis. 'Re-establishing our relationship is more important than dwelling on our past mistakes.'

Having been taken aback by that sudden flash of anger, Lara turned away, as pale and shaken as though a shark had leapt out of a tranquil pond in front of her. She had been ridiculously naïve, she thought painfully, to think that all was forgotten and forgiven. Evidently, he had put the blame on her, and she was tempted to round on him and give him her frank opinion of what he had done and said to drive her from his side. But Gaetano had been quite correct in that this was neither the time nor the place to dive into the swamp of the past. Everything was too new and fresh between them, and it would be wiser to concentrate on the present than risk destructive recriminations.

That afternoon, a stylist arrived to take her clothing measurements, Gaetano having pointed out that she would require what he described as a 'more flexible wardrobe'. By the time the stylist had moved on from measurements to requesting her colour and fashion preferences, even Gaetano's subtle approach had warned Lara that she was really receiving a makeover. She joined Gaetano, Alice and Dario for dinner in a lofty-ceilinged formal dining room where they were waited on as if they were…well, royalty.

She learned from a question that Alice asked that this was Gaetano's very first visit to the house he had inherited three years earlier. As her friend raised her brows in her direction, Lara knew exactly what Alice was thinking. Who on earth inherited a giant house from their grandfather, unknown or otherwise, and waited three years to visit it? And only then because it was convenient to where he wanted to be? Someone who might well own a lot of property, someone from a world entirely removed from theirs in every way…

Alice studied Lara when she accompanied her back to her bedroom where Iris already slept in one of the twin beds. 'You really have jumped in with both feet again with him, haven't you?'

'Yes, there's just something about Gaetano which blasts all common sense right out of my head,' Lara conceded wryly. 'I'm still insanely attached to him.'

Alice laughed. 'Well, I'm not sure I would

call it insane. He's filthy rich, devastatingly handsome, very entertaining and he's a king. He does also seem incredibly keen to be married to you again.'

'It feels a bit too much like a fairy tale,' Lara whispered worriedly.

'You really do *deserve* the fairy tale,' her friend told her softly.

Gaetano wasn't there when she got ready for bed in the grand bedroom that they had shared that afternoon. He had mentioned having allowed work to pile up while he came to England to visit her. She felt alone, though, and scolded herself for it. Of course, Gaetano, the monarch, had many more responsibilities than the guy with amnesia she had first met, who had been able to devote himself unreservedly to her. My goodness, without even appreciating that truth, she had been spoilt by him!

The acknowledgement made her buck up and accept reality. He would give her and Freddy what time he had to give, and she would make the best of it for the sake of their marriage. She fell asleep feeling lonely but comforted by the pious reminder that there was no such thing as perfect in any marriage...

CHAPTER SEVEN

THE FOLLOWING AFTERNOON, Gaetano, Lara and Freddy flew to Mosvakia. She barely recognised her own reflection in the luxury washroom on the private jet. Her glamorous powder-blue knee-length dress and light matching coat teamed with toning shoes looked incredibly elegant, although nothing could have prepared Lara for the pomp and ceremony that greeted their arrival.

'Why didn't you warn me?' she gasped, as Gaetano urged her down the steps from the jet to the crowds awaiting them.

Some people were waving with enthusiasm. Many were wielding cameras. Yet more were arranged in a formal line to greet them. Off to one side a regimental band was playing an upbeat thundering tune. The smiles and the music went some way towards banishing her immediate attack of stage fright. It was a celebration, not something to fear, she registered, the tightness in her chest receding and her breath coming a little easier.

A wave of introductions followed on the tarmac, the prime minister, the chief of staff of the army and that of the police force. Those were just some of the people she met. An eye-catchingly beautiful woman with long black hair and bright blue eyes disconcerted Lara by immediately mentioning that she was an ex-girlfriend of Gaetano's.

'Although I'm afraid there are all too many of us in *that* category!' she joked with such wide-eyed amusement that Lara could only admire her good nature. Her name was Antonella. 'I'm so happy that Gaetano has found a wife and now he has a son as well. How wonderful! I currently have an intern position at the palace, so you'll see me again. I do hope we can be friends.'

'I don't see why not,' Lara responded, charmed by that frank speech as Gaetano's hand at her spine urged her on down the line.

'What did Antonella have to say to you that took so long?' Gaetano enquired.

In surprise, Lara glanced up at him and immediately recognised the faint tension etched in his lean darkly handsome features, tightening his high cheekbones and bracketing his narrowed golden gaze. 'Nothing much. She seemed charming.'

'Oh, she is,' Gaetano agreed calmly. 'She's the prime minister's daughter, quite a privileged young woman.'

Someone else grabbed his attention and that was the end of the conversation. Lara had wanted to ask when he had dated Antonella but, on reflection, decided that that would be an unwise enquiry. How would she feel if he told her he had been seeing the beautiful woman during their marriage? And that was perfectly possible, wasn't it? She suppressed the sense of insecurity assailing her. She didn't want to turn into an insanely jealous woman, did she?

After all, whether she liked it or not, she had been the one to walk out on their marriage. It was even possible that she had misread Gaetano's signals that day. She didn't want to think that about herself. She didn't want to think that she could have made such a ghastly mistake about *his* feelings for her. Even so, the anger he had revealed about her disappearance from his life only a day earlier had forced her to wonder whether she had misinterpreted his reaction to their marriage after he had regained his memory.

'You're very quiet. There won't usually be this amount of interest in us, but the marriage announcement two years after the event and Freddy's existence were bound to attract attention,' Gaetano pointed out in an effort to be soothing, because at the back of his mind he still had the fear that if Lara was thrust too fast and too deep into the limelight, which she didn't want in the first place, she might vanish on him again. It was foolish, he told himself, but, nonetheless, that fear was alive and well just about every time he looked at her. He needed to put that anxiety behind him. He didn't fuss over women; he didn't normally worry about them either. Why was she so different?

'So, why did you call Antonella "privileged"?' Lara heard herself ask, although she had promised herself that she would not ask Gaetano a single question about his ex-girlfriend. Her curiosity betrayed her, however.

'Her sense of entitlement and confidence have ruffled feathers on the household staff,' Gaetano confided. 'But to be fair to her, the staff *are* behind the times. My brother preferred the old ways in every sphere but I'm of the younger generation. Antonella does all the PR and she's the first in that position.'

Lara let the subject drop, relieved of any further concern by Gaetano's relaxed response and explanation.

The limousine was driving now at a slower stately pace down a long steep driveway surrounded by trees. When the trees finally parted, she saw an elegant white building on a hill. Adorned with castellated towers, it bore a remarkable resemblance to a jigsaw of a fairy-tale castle she had once done as a child. Several different storeys climbed the slope. Beautifully manicured terraced gardens surrounded Gaetano's home.

As her nerves began to nibble at her composure, she breathed in deep. Freddy, who was in top form after meeting so many strangers and receiving smiles and appreciation from them all, squealed with excitement. Gaetano dismissed the offer of assistance from one of the half-dozen hovering staff eager to help and reached in to lift his son out of the limousine himself. As Freddy squirmed in the grip of one arm, he closed his free arm round Lara's small trembling frame with all the firmness of a prison guard.

'No need to glad-hand anyone here. This is our home and we're heading straight to our private apartments,' he intoned half under his breath before he fixed a polite smile to his darkly handsome face and forged a path through the gathering crowd to take them indoors.

Lara's eyes glazed over in the vast echoing hall where towering, majestic mirrors and chandeliers offered a myriad reflections of people awaiting their arrival.

'My wife is very tired.' Gaetano excused them smoothly, urging her across the hall into a lift while signalling their nanny.

'I'm not that tired,' Lara muttered apologetically as Gaetano lowered Freddy to the floor in the corridor they stepped into.

Gaetano stepped round her to speak to the nanny and suggest that she take their son to the nursery.

'Gaetano, I was planning—' she began uncomfortably.

He closed a hand over hers in a gesture that brooked no argument and urged her down the corridor and into a room with giant double doors. 'Our bedroom,' he told her. 'Be grateful for the modern furniture. When my brother was alive, it was the same as it was in my great-grandfather's day with a massive four-poster. It gave me the creeps. Giulia refurnished it for me. She did a lot of redecoration after losing Vittorio. It gave her something to do. However, you are free to change anything and everything in this wing of the palace. It is now *our* home.'

'That's good to know,' Lara mumbled, still shaken by a bedroom the size of a football pitch with numerous connecting doors. It was exquisitely decorated in shades of soft blue and green with touches of white. 'But I shouldn't think I'd want to change anything in here. It's stunning as it is.'

'It's a shame that Giulia has moved abroad. You would have liked her.'

'You must miss her too.'

'Yes, but now I have a family again,' he reminded her, his lean hands lifting to curve to her shoulders, long brown fingers flexing against her slender bones in a caressing motion.

'I was going to spend time with Freddy,' she murmured.

'You've been with Freddy all day, now *I* want a piece of your time,' Gaetano husked as he gazed down at her with mesmeric golden eyes under a canopy of lush black lashes. 'Freddy has an entire nursery staff at his disposal and it's not as though our son is shy or clingy, is it?'

'No, it's not. He's like you…full of himself,' she teased with a sudden helpless smile because when Gaetano looked at her in a certain way, the rest of the world just vanished along with every other concern.

'And I'm allowed the occasional piece of you too,' Gaetano reasoned huskily, tipping the coat off her shoulders and turning her around to run down the zip on the dress. 'When I came to bed last night you were asleep and I had an early morning phone call I had to rise to take. That happens a lot in my life: I can't do what I want to do.'

'I suppose it goes with the job,' Lara mused as her dress hit the splendid woven rug below her feet.

'But now I have a private life and a good reason to free myself up more often,' Gaetano pointed out.

'I'm quite sure you had a private social

life *before* you found out where I was living,' Lara returned quietly, wanting there to be no secrets between them and that included topics that she might feel that she preferred to avoid.

Gaetano straightened as he scooped her up and laid her down on the wide bed. 'I haven't had a single social engagement outside what I consider to be work.'

Lara's brows knitted. It worried her that he didn't feel he could be honest with her. 'I did walk out on our marriage but then I did assume that, as Dario had said, it couldn't have been legal for you to marry me without your brother's consent.'

'I have to admit that I don't even recall Dario saying anything of that nature,' Gaetano admitted as he wrenched off his tie and then paused to reflect on her words. 'I was so devastated to hear of my brother's sudden death that I barely recollect anything that anyone said that morning. I knew his illness was terminal, but I assumed he would be with us for many months more. Vittorio was virtually my father, and I had no other family. And the realisation that I was to become

King without any warning…well, to be brutally honest, it *overwhelmed* me.'

It was a moment of truth for Lara. She had been too busy that day seeing her own cosy little world with Gaetano destroyed to acknowledge the traumatic news that Gaetano had received at the same time. Although she had had all the facts, she had not put them together then, or afterwards, she conceded with regret. The sad truth was that both she and Gaetano had been too preoccupied with their separate concerns to think sensibly about their marriage.

'And *I* was overwhelmed by who you really were,' she confided belatedly, sliding off the bed to brush his stilled fingers away and efficiently unbutton his shirt. 'Realising that you were rich and royal, and that you had this whole other important life in another country, scared the life out of me.'

'But you're not so scared now, are you?'

Lara fumbled with his cufflinks. 'I'm working on it. I'm a bit gutsier now than I was back then.'

'Stronger,' Gaetano agreed with a smile. 'I like that.'

'You may not like it so much if I ever dare

to use it against you,' Lara contended with a glint in her aquamarine eyes.

'Would you?' he asked, shedding his shirt, toeing off his shoes, bending to peel off his socks. 'Because two years ago, you wouldn't have.'

'Without you, I toughened up.'

Gaetano tugged her into his arms. 'I like strong, independent women,' he declared, crushing her parted lips hungrily with his, his breath fanning her cheek as he slid her back onto the bed with single-minded purpose.

'I'm talking too much,' she guessed.

Gaetano laughed and grinned down at her. 'I missed your honesty but I'm not quite sure I like the fact that you can read me so well. I've never met anyone else with that ability and occasionally, it's unnerving.'

'You said it, Your Majesty,' Lara whispered, running her hands down the sides of his lean thighs and then sending them up to rove across his hard stomach and his firm pectorals as she sat up and claimed his mouth again for herself. Every nerve in her body thrilled to that connection.

He groaned into her mouth, momentarily rigid with sexual hunger against her and it whisked her back in time because his response to her had not changed in the slightest. With impatient hands he removed the silk and lace lingerie she still wore. 'I can't get enough of you now, *bambola*,' he assured her feverishly.

'I think I can live with frequent ravishment.' She laughed.

Gaetano spread her out on the bed as though she were a feast to be savoured. Expert hands traced her slender ribcage up to the pouting fullness of her breasts and tugged on the delicate peaks. He lowered his mouth there to toy with her until her hips began to shift and rise, the liquid heat at her core making her restless. She wanted more…oh, *how* she wanted more, she reflected, helpless in the grip of the craving he was awakening inside her. He traced the delicate folds between her thighs and used his carnal mouth and fingers to incite a fire of need. For a long time, he teased her until her whole body was trembling on the sharp edge of delight. When a climax engulfed her in a blaze of intense pleasure she writhed and moaned.

'You are the hottest, sexiest woman on this earth,' Gaetano groaned into her hair, sliding over her and into her in one sleek, hard thrust of power.

A surge of renewed hunger washed through her as he pushed her knees back to deepen his invasion. Her body jolted with the driving power of his possession. Every nerve ending reacted, firing her response with an immediacy that was incredibly exciting. Her heart was racing, her blood rushing in her veins and then the excitement peaked for her, drowning her in blissful sensation until she lay limp.

As Gaetano released her Lara rolled onto him, determined to retain that intimacy. 'I want a hug,' she told him saucily.

And his immediate smile chased all the gravity from his lean darkly handsome face, his dark eyes tawny gold with satisfaction below the tousled black hair on his brow. My word, he was beautiful, she thought abstractedly, tracing the fullness of his pink lower lip, emphasised by the black veil of stubble beginning to frame it.

He closed his arms round her and she felt safe and secure the way only he had ever made her feel. She wanted to tell him that she still loved him, but she held the words back because she felt that it was far too soon to be that honest.

The next day she explored their enormous private wing, amused to discover that it spanned three floors and countless rooms as well as enjoying access to a private garden. Certainly, space was unlikely to be a problem for them. Gaetano had an office in the top of one of the towers, a book-lined refuge. She popped her head round the door, saw Dario was with him and went into instant retreat.

'No, join us for coffee,' Gaetano insisted, yanking open the door again before she could escape.

Dario pulled out a chair for her and she sat down, a diminutive figure clad in a green sweater and leggings. Gaetano laughed. 'You look like an elf in that colour. We have to fill in some forms to apply to have Freddy's birth certificate altered and brought up to date.'

As the forms were settled in front of her, Lara scrawled her signature, a guilty grimace etched on her face. 'I wish I had named you on the certificate and owned up to our marriage.'

'We'll get it sorted out eventually,' Gaetano said bracingly, squeezing her shoulder and urging her back into her seat. 'Don't worry about it.'

'You'll have a fabulous time in Morocco,' Dario remarked.

Gaetano frowned at his friend. 'Thank you, Dario, for breaking the news.'

Lara's eyes had widened. 'Morocco?'

'A belated honeymoon, the least of what I owe you,' Gaetano told her with a slow smile. 'We leave at the end of the week.'

'Freddy—?'

'He's my son too. I wasn't planning to leave him behind.' Gaetano studied her with amusement as she poured the coffee.

A knock sounded on the door and a tall blond man strode in, greeting Gaetano with enthusiasm. For a couple of minutes they spoke in French and then Gaetano swung him round with a smile and introduced him. 'Lara, meet Olivier Laurent. He's a renowned photographer and a good friend from my schooldays. I invited him here to take some photographs of you and Freddy. If we release official photos, it gives the paparazzi less reason to sneak up on us,' he explained.

Lara stood up to be kissed French fashion on either cheek. Olivier didn't have a reserved bone in his body, it seemed, as he grabbed her hands, set her back from him and looked her over with a professional eye that had a flirty twinkle. 'You've done very well, Gaetano. I work with models who would kill for that glowing complexion and that combination of hair and eyes.'

'Thanks.' Lara straightened her shoulders.

'You said to make it an informal session,' Olivier reminded Gaetano. 'I like your wife dressed just as she is but she may want to gild the lily first.'

'You want to do this now?' Lara asked, because as far as gilding the lily went she had already applied make-up from the giant box of cosmetics she had received along with her new and vast wardrobe, which contained outfits to cover every possible occasion. 'Because I'm fine as I am.'

'Put on your rings or earrings at least,' Olivier advised.

'We'll be back in a few minutes,' Gaetano murmured, his high cheekbones scored with colour as he closed a hand to hers and urged her out of the room.

'Where are we going?'

'I've been very remiss. I haven't even *given*

you any jewellery!' Gaetano ground out in a guilt-stricken undertone. 'What sort of a husband am I?'

'Well, you were only a husband for six weeks and I wouldn't let you spend what you had on stuff we didn't truly need, then we had the break and I've only been back in your life for a few days. Luckily, I kept my wedding ring even if I didn't wear it until this week,' Lara pointed out soothingly. 'Let's not fuss about the little things.'

Gaetano took her into another room and opened a safe, carting out a towering pile of jewellery boxes while Lara looked on in wonderment. 'The trouble is that all this is antique and family stuff.'

'I don't need to wear your family's jewellery, for goodness' sake,' Lara protested in embarrassment.

'All of this is yours to wear as my wife. I'll buy you your own pieces when we have the time but Olivier's right…it would look odd in the photos if you wore no jewellery at all.'

'I don't care if I look like a bargain-basement bride,' Lara told him with a chuckle.

'But *I do*,' Gaetano shot back at her in a raw undertone. 'In marrying me, you lost out every step of the way. You had to borrow your wedding dress because you wouldn't agree to me buying you one. You had no party, no engagement ring, no honeymoon, not one single thing that other brides take for granted!'

'Things like that are not important to me. It's feelings that matter. Our wedding was very romantic,' she reminded him softly. 'Snow on the ground, just you and me and Dr Beresford and her husband. I *loved* my borrowed dress. I thought the whole day was magical.'

Gaetano stared back at her in amazement, his stunning dark golden eyes still troubled. 'Honestly?'

'Honestly,' Lara confirmed with a smile. 'I didn't have a family to invite and the only close friends I had weren't available. We were together. That was all that mattered.'

With visible difficulty, Gaetano dragged his eyes back from her lovely face and began snapping open several ring boxes. 'Pick a couple…' he invited.

'Oh, that's gorgeous!' Lara prised a beautiful solitaire diamond out of a box and tried it on her finger beside the wedding ring. 'And as it fits it was obviously meant to be!'

'It was my grandmother's… I believe. She was gone before my birth, but Vittorio and Giulia once sat me down to talk me through all this stuff and its provenance. Somewhere there is an official catalogue. Try another ring and some earrings,' he encouraged.

Lara slid a square-cut sapphire dress ring on her other hand.

All the earrings he unveiled were either too fancy or for pierced ears and her ears were unpierced, so Gaetano had to be satisfied with the rings now adorning her fingers.

Lara collected Freddy from the nursery. Like her, he had enjoyed a wardrobe refresh and he looked adorable in embroidered dungarees and a matching sweater. Olivier met them at the foot of the stairs and said to Gaetano, 'I can take it from here and you can go back to work. I've been using the palace as a backdrop for portraits for long enough to know all the best locations.'

'I'll stay. I haven't seen much of Freddy today,' Gaetano announced.

Olivier definitely seemed to know what he was doing behind a camera, giving her detailed instructions of how to pose, where to look, with slick directions and amusing comments that made her relax and laugh more than once. They had to be a little more active to please Freddy and keep him in one place long enough to be photographed.

'I'm really enjoying winding Gaetano up,' Olivier murmured quietly after an hour as he bent down to Freddy's level and play-fought the little boy to make him chuckle. 'I've never seen him so gone on a woman that he would stand around watching just to make sure I don't get *too* friendly with her!' Laughing with satisfaction, he backed away from mother and son again.

It was frustrating for Lara not to be able to look around right at that moment to see if Gaetano really was there watching. Olivier was an old friend and his frank words lifted her to a height. The idea that Gaetano could be recapturing some of the emotion she had once inspired in him was extremely appealing now that she had accepted that she was as much in love with him today as she had been two years earlier.

The main difference between then and now was that she understood how much more complex a character Gaetano was than she had once assumed. And how volatile he could be, she acknowledged ruefully, beneath the hard shell of equable cool that his royal role had imposed on him. Without knowing who and what he really was, she hadn't grasped what that conflict in his nature meant, nor had she been aware that she and Freddy saw a side of him that few other people, if any, had had the benefit of experiencing.

Gaetano had a flinty darkness to his gaze when he gathered her up after the session ended and Freddy was borne off to have his supper by his nanny. 'You should have told Olivier to back off,' he breathed unreasonably.

Lara lifted a brow. 'He's a happily married man with two kids. You can't be serious. He was winding you up deliberately.'

Gaetano frowned and stiffened. '*Stai scherzando*...are you kidding me? I felt that he was being disrespectful.'

'No, not at all,' Lara disagreed. 'He's a friend and he was teasing you.'

Gaetano gritted his teeth and said nothing more. Seeing Olivier, one of the worst womanisers in Europe before his marriage, getting that close to Lara had inflamed him. Clearly, Lara liked Olivier—well, most women did, he conceded grudgingly. But the more she had laughed and responded to Olivier's undoubted charms, the angrier Gaetano had felt. Obviously, he was a rather territorial man, who preferred that other men respect clear boundaries rather than flirt with his wife in front of him. There was nothing wrong with that. Olivier had been in the wrong, *not* him.

'Oh, yes, Dario's wife, Carla, is dying to meet you and I said we'd drop in on them later for supper,' Gaetano imparted. 'She's very friendly and warm. I think you'll like her.'

'Would you have a minute?' Antonella asked Lara as she was walking through the big hall towards the lift, intending to join Freddy in the nursery.

'There's some ideas I wanted to run by you. Mosvakia needs to meet their new queen properly,' she told Lara cheerfully as she invited her into one of the offices on the ground floor.

Lara swallowed hard, recalling how Gaetano had promised her that she only had to be a queen behind closed doors. 'Is it really important? I don't want to put myself out there if I don't have to.'

'You and Gaetano are a double act. How could you not appreciate that he needs your support?' Antonella asked in almost exaggerated surprise. 'Charities and other organisations, not to mention the government's scheduled events, require more time than the King has in his day. You could relieve some of the pressure on him by taking on some of those duties.'

Lara had paled. She levelled her shoulders, trying to stand taller because, although she was accustomed to being smaller than most of the people around her, inexplicably Antonella made her feel like a small person on the inside as well as the outside. 'Of course, I'll help if I can,' she murmured limply, terrified that she was being selfish and determined to make Gaetano proud of her. Antonella's surprise made it obvious that skulking behind closed doors was not going to impress anyone. 'I didn't appreciate that Gaetano was under so much pressure. This is early days for us.'

'The King works very hard. When I was with him…oh, forgive me.' Antonella studied her with an apologetic grimace. 'I meant not to remind you of that. It just slid off my tongue.'

'Don't worry about it. I'm well aware that I'm not the only woman whom Gaetano has had in his life,' Lara managed to respond in an upbeat tone, resolute, as she was, not to be oversensitive, but perhaps it *was* time for her to talk to Gaetano more honestly about the time they had spent apart rather than dancing round the sticky subject and avoiding it. In some cases, such as right there at that very moment, ignorance was not bliss.

'Well, of course, I knew the King before you entered his life,' Antonella began in a remorseful tone.

'Before?' Lara queried, her spine snapping rigid with sudden fierce tension. *'Before?'* she repeated helplessly.

'I'm sorry. I assumed he would have mentioned it by now. We were dating before he disappeared the way he did.' Antonella had lowered her voice. 'I only know about *that* episode because my father is Prime Minister. For obvious reasons, it's been kept very quiet. He forgot that he already had a girlfriend, but I can hardly complain when he had a medical reason for doing so.'

'My goodness,' Lara exclaimed in response to that revelation. She contrived a stiff smile and struggled to maintain her composure when, in actuality, she felt as though she had received a hard punch in the stomach. 'That must have been very difficult for you. Do you mind me asking how close you were?'

Already regretting asking such an intimate question, Lara watched Antonella bend her head, her face colouring. 'I don't think we should get into that, but I was like any other woman in a relationship with a man of the King's standing... I did hope that it was a lasting bond, of course I did. And unfortunately, nothing was explained when he first came back, and he stayed away from me. *Nobody* knew that the King had married—well, possibly Dario did, but the rest of us didn't. That was a very well-kept secret.'

'I'm so sorry you had that experience,' Lara murmured tightly. 'Look, Freddy's waiting on me. Could we discuss those events you mentioned on some other day?'

'Of course, Your Majesty. Get back to me when you have a free moment,' Antonella urged with a pleasant smile.

She's a nice person, Lara reasoned, why do

I feel as if I hate her? Why do I feel as if she has destroyed me?

But it wasn't Antonella's fault that she had brought something to light that neither Gaetano nor Lara had considered two years earlier. Why hadn't they considered that he might have another woman in his life? Indeed, that he might even be in a relationship with someone else? On the only occasion when Lara *had* mentioned that possibility, Gaetano had outright laughed at the suggestion, insisting that he could never ever have forgotten someone that important to him. And she had believed that, hadn't she? Because it had suited her to do so, her conscience pointed out. Madly in love as she had been and Gaetano had *seemed* to be, the idea that he might owe loyalty to another woman would have been a devastating blow to her warmest hopes and prayers.

But for Gaetano, how much worse would it have been had he remembered that he *loved* that other woman the moment he regained his memory?

And wasn't that, bearing in mind his tension when he had seen her talking to Antonella, the more likely scenario?

After all, Antonella was absolutely gorgeous, like one of those supermodels you saw and lingered on in a glossy magazine. She was well educated, Mosvakian and from a good background. In short, Antonella was everything that Lara was not, and she was painfully conscious of the differences between them.

Gaetano had said he had not enjoyed a single happy moment since she had left their marriage, she reminded herself in desperation. But hadn't Gaetano originally approached her looking for a divorce? And hadn't his attitude only changed after Freddy entered their relationship and he accepted him? Freddy, the Crown Prince, their son, who was so much more important in Mosvakia than Lara in her naivety had ever appreciated. Freddy was treated in the palace like a precious jewel. Young though he was, Freddy was viewed as a future king. Here in the palace his outgoing nature was much admired. Freddy was a vital element in their marriage. Without *his* existence would Gaetano still have wanted her back?

Such damaging fears would normally have sent Lara to bed early but instead she

had to head out with Gaetano to visit Dario and Carla's town house. Engulfed by Carla's lively tribe of pet dogs, however, there was no time to brood. Carla was much more outgoing and casual than her husband and, not being a Mosvakian by birth, she didn't have his reverent attitude to the monarchy. To her surprise, Lara thoroughly enjoyed the evening and noticed how much more relaxed and likeable Dario was in his wife's company.

Lara was remembering the last time her trust in Gaetano had been tested, two years earlier, and she had run away sooner than stand her ground like an adult. She was no longer that immature and insecure, she reasoned with herself. He deserved the benefit of the doubt this time around.

She might want to confront Gaetano about Antonella, but how could she confront a man who might well have done nothing wrong? Who had had every *right* to be in love with another woman when he first met Lara even if he couldn't remember the fact? That wrying question kept her lips sealed for following two days while she strugg'behave normally.

CHAPTER EIGHT

FLYING ON HIS private jet to Morocco with his family, Gaetano was brimming with dissatisfaction.

He had accepted the ugly truth that in the husband stakes he had been a disaster. He was proud that he had the humility to acknowledge that reality and he was fully committed to rectifying his mistakes. Sadly, for him, however, Lara was no longer on the same wavelength. For the very first time in his life, he was at a loss with a woman and his recently awakened conscience did not prevent him from seething with angry frustration when his attempts to improve the situation met a solid brick wall of indifference.

For the past forty-eight hours, Lara had been more distant than the Himalayas. She emanated an invisible but highly effective forcefield that repelled him. Even in bed, surely the ultimate insult, he reflected grimly, thinking of how she had muttered about how tired she was before taking refuge at the farthest edge of the bed as though he were some kind of sex fiend she was desperate to avoid.

Lara's real problem, however, was that she was hopeless at hiding anything from him. Her smiles were stiff, her voice expressionless, her eyes unwilling to meet his. That something had gone wrong pretty much screamed from Lara. Unfortunately, she was married to a guy who was too clever by far to *ever* ask a woman what was wrong and receive some bitten off passive-aggressive 'Fine' in response.

But slowly and steadily, nonetheless, Lara was driving Gaetano up the wall. Worse still, her behaviour had *shocked* him. Gaetano, who had fondly believed that he was shock-proof with women. And yet here was Lara, whom he had truly believed was above such games, and she was shocking him with her detachment. *Shutting him out.* He couldn't stand it; he genuinely couldn't stand it. And it didn't help that he didn't know why, didn't understand why such a change in her attitude could affect him to such an extent when no woman before her had had the ability to affect his mood.

Of course, he was accustomed to her warmth and her acceptance, and no woman had ever had the power to make him relax the way Lara did. When that was suddenly withdrawn without explanation, naturally he would feel troubled. While he had been taught to suppress his emotions, he still couldn't manage that feat around Lara, and when one distant glance from Lara bothered him, his own overreaction made him feel out of control because he wasn't accustomed to handling the turmoil inside him.

Maybe she had somehow got him hooked on all that touchy-feely cuddling she was so keen on. Certainly, he wasn't stupid. He was aware that he had never had that sort of warmth from any other woman, not that it hadn't been offered, only that he had once had the good sense to refuse that kind of empty, inappropriate affection. But Lara's affection hadn't felt empty or inappropriate or fake. And weirdly, he *missed* it. All of it: the hand slipping into his, the hugs, the appreciative smiles, the laughter like liquid sunshine that revitalised him. His shapely mouth flattened and compressed. The awareness and the thought that had led to it only increased his annoyance. *Madre di Dio*…she now had him agonising over stuff as if he were a teenage girl!

As they climbed into an SUV at Marrakech Menara airport, Lara was painfully aware that she was handling what she had learned from Antonella very badly. Sadly, Antonella had struck a killing blow because Lara deeply cherished her memories of that first six weeks with Gaetano during which she had fallen in love with and married him. Antonella had struck at the very roots of that precious emotional history and squashed her flat. If the other woman was telling the truth, Gaetano had never been Lara's except by default and his love had never been real even at the beginning, indeed, could only have been an infatuation caused by circumstance. And that hurt, good grief, that *really* hurt, Lara acknowledged unhappily.

'Where are we staying?' she enquired to break the awful silence that had fallen between her and Gaetano long before they left the palace.

'At the Palais des Roses property my grand-father built in the swinging sixties. The estate lies on the outskirts of the city. As a child I came here for regular holidays with Vittorio.'

'Not Giulia?'

'I was already an adult by the time my brother married Giulia. Her parents were family friends, though, and often visited the palace when I was a teenager. That's when I watched movies with her. Vittorio had several ill-fated relationships with women and, with everyone keen to see him marry and carry on the family line, he finally settled on Giulia because she was a safe choice—'

'That's sad.'

Gaetano frowned. 'It would have been even sadder if Vittorio had made the mistake of choosing a bride who only wanted him for his wealth and status. My mother married my father for his position and Vittorio watched that car crash happen. It made him very wary. Once my mother established that Mosvakia was not *the* most fashionable place to be, she spent her time socialising in London with her friends. I was born there because she didn't want to return to Mosvakia.'

Having left the buzzing, busy city behind,

their convoy of cars was driving through olive groves. Soon enough they were surrounded on all sides by a plantation of soaring date palms and Lara carefully confined her attention to the view from the car windows. The SUV only slowed down when an impossibly long expanse of tall white wall appeared. The wall was divided by massive wrought-iron gates, which were swung open by two beaming older men.

A glorious wash of exquisite pastel-coloured roses in brimming beds encircled the driveway and she stepped out into the sunshine. A horseshoe arch led into a courtyard with pillars and a tiled floor sprinkled with rose petals to welcome their arrival. Water was running somewhere nearby, and a healthy collection of evergreen shrubs and small trees vied for her attention in the flower beds.

She was ushered straight into a room so packed with striking colourful features that she simply stared, taking in intricate kilim-upholstered seating, elaborate plasterwork, a carved wooden painted ceiling, and spectacular mosaic tiles applied to shoulder height on the walls. 'My word, it's like some *Arabian Nights* fantasy.'

'It's a house of curiosities,' Gaetano said wryly, urging her in the direction of the concealed staircase at the rear of the room. 'My grandfather spent years building it with teams of master craftsmen and ran himself deep into debt. Like my father, he was extravagant.'

'There's fireplaces everywhere,' Lara remarked, glancing into another room as they passed it. 'I wasn't expecting that.'

'Desert nights are chilly once the sun goes down.' On the floor above, he walked her out onto a giant roof terrace that contained a gleaming swimming pool, plants in massive colourful urns and loads of outside seating. 'In summer we lived mostly outdoors here.'

'It sounds idyllic…and the view is out of this world,' Lara remarked as she leant on the retaining wall, gazing out at the snow-capped Atlas Mountain range backing the seemingly endless expanse of dense date palms. 'Much more lush and green than I was expecting.'

'When are you planning to tell me what's wrong?' Gaetano shot at her with an unexpectedness that jolted her.

Lara spun round, clashing with scorching dark eyes that seared her, and she lost colour. 'I don't know what you're talking—'

'Quit while you're ahead. You can't act for peanuts. For the past two days you have been treating me like the invisible man when we're out of bed and a potential degenerate when we're in it!'

Taken aback by that full-frontal attack and his anger, Lara stared back at him, her cheeks red with heat and her chest heaving as she sucked in oxygen to fill her compressed lungs. For a moment she couldn't find her voice.

'Did Olivier say something about me that annoyed or offended you?' Gaetano prompted in a low intense tone. 'I noticed that your attitude to me changed after *his* visit…and if you don't come clean right now, Lara, I intend to phone him.'

'Don't you *dare*!' Lara snapped back at him in dismay. 'It's nothing to do with Olivier. He said not one word out of place about you.'

His lean, strikingly handsome face merely tightened. 'That is good to know, because he's a close friend. But it annoys me that you feel that you cannot speak freely to me. Am I so intimidating? So untrustworthy that you can't simply be frank with me?'

Shame and regret filled Lara and an uneasy

silence stretched as a tray of refreshments was brought out to the terrace by a member of the staff.

Gaetano thanked the older woman in French and introduced her to Lara. 'This is our housekeeper, Maryam. Her husband, Ahmed, is our cook.'

The mint tea was poured, and tiny pastries offered. Lara was too overwrought to be capable of eating anything. She sipped the sweet herbal tea and nibbled at the edge of a pastry to pass herself below Maryam's anxious scrutiny while wondering if the older woman had heard their raised voices. Inside herself she was dying a thousand deaths of embarrassment.

'I'm not very good at confrontation, but that doesn't matter because you haven't done *anything* wrong,' she stressed uncomfortably as soon as Maryam had vanished indoors again.

'Then what on earth has caused this change in you?' Gaetano demanded rawly.

'Something Antonella let drop,' she muttered reluctantly.

'Antonella?' Gaetano's mouth took on a

sardonic curve and his dark golden eyes hardened. 'Why does that not surprise me?'

Lara sank down on a cushioned seat because her legs felt weak. 'I was a bit shocked because she mentioned that you and she had been dating *before* you had your fall that Christmas with me two years ago.'

'*Dating?* That's news to me,' Gaetano countered thinly, incensed colour lining his hard cheekbones. 'Her father brought us together on a trip to the opera house, and then on another occasion I was invited to a dinner by a friend and discovered that I was expected to partner Antonella. Neither event was a date and, in any case, in my position, I would have to be pretty stupid to get involved with the daughter of a politician. I have always given the daughters of our local dignitaries a wide berth. In fact, I have never had an affair with a woman in Mosvakia. Since I was a teenager, it was easier and safer to enjoy such freedoms abroad.'

'That's quite a speech.'

'Evidently a necessary one,' Gaetano condemned. 'Do you honestly think that I would allow an ex to work in the palace and work closely with my wife? I'm more sensible than that, although I have to say that you seem to be less than sensible on the same topic. What else did Antonella tell you?'

'Well…' Lara floundered. 'It wasn't so much what she said as the impression she gave me…that you and she had been very close.'

'Nonsense,' he dismissed without hesitation. 'I'm skilled at being courteous and nothing more to women keen to attract my attention when I have no intention of reciprocating. That's been an element of my life since school. You're too trusting, Lara. You should have brought this concern straight to me. I'll put Dario onto finding another location for Antonella.'

'Oh, don't do that—not if it's likely to cause offence to her family.'

'I don't like troublemakers, *bambola*…or the streak of spite Antonella has revealed. She lied to you. We weren't dating. There has never been any physical contact between us. What other stories might she weave? There was no *other* woman in my life when I first met you. Plainly, Antonella hit out at you because *I* had injured her ego. I won't have her anywhere near you now that she's shown her true colours.'

A slow smile curved Lara's formerly tense mouth. He was so protective that he made her toes curl. Even two years ago, clueless about his identity, Gaetano had been driven by that same compassionate strength. Not since her father's death had she been able to rely on a man and her experiences as a teen, forced to live with the ever-changing turmoil of her mother's love life, had made her wary and distrustful of men before she met him.

'I should've trusted you, at least given you the benefit of the doubt,' she conceded, pained that she had believed every word that fell from the other woman's lips. 'I've wasted two days fretting about something that never happened.'

Gaetano reached for her hands and held fast to them. 'I don't like it when you close me out.'

'I'm not used to having anyone I can talk to in a crisis,' Lara confided. 'I was never free to honestly talk to Alice about us because she's hopeless at keeping secrets.'

Shimmering dark golden eyes held hers. Her mouth ran dry, and her tummy flipped with the force of her sexual awareness. He wound long fingers slowly into several strands of wavy strawberry hair, watching how the fading sunlight lit it up to a peach shade. 'I'm used to keeping my own counsel, so I have to admit talking is a challenge for me as well.'

Her hand tugged free of his to curve to one lean cheekbone, her fingertips stroking his olive skin. 'In other words, we are both useless at communication.' She sighed.

Gaetano burst out laughing. 'I love the way you find fault with me.'

Black lashes dipping low over piercing eyes, he scooped her up into his arms. 'It is much easier to kiss you lying down, *bambola mia*,' he explained.

'Is that your excuse?' Lara was thinking that Gaetano had never had the smallest problem in communicating his needs. He was innately powerful, persuasive and driven to succeed.

His stunning eyes flared down into hers. 'Do I need one?'

'No.'

Her heart raced as he claimed her parted lips ravenously with his own, his tongue delving deep as he carried her indoors to the blessed cool. That electrifying shock effect lit up every nerve ending in her body. She trembled against him as he rested her down on a bed and joined her there to continue kissing her with driving hunger. Nothing had ever felt so good or so necessary as the restoration of that physical connection.

As they both paused to draw breath, Lara looked up at him anxiously. 'I don't want to be asking you awkward questions about what happened in your life while we were apart. I know I walked out on you…as you see it. I accept that…morally speaking, you felt that you were free to do whatever you liked with other women.'

Gaetano stared down at her with troubled dark eyes. 'I never felt that way. I knew I was married. I knew I wasn't free. I don't cheat, Lara. My mother cheated on my father and a couple of Vittorio's girlfriends cheated on him. It's painful and humiliating. I haven't been with anyone but you since the day we exchanged our vows,' he admitted tautly.

Lara gazed back at him in shock and surprise and a great floodtide of relief washed through her, her aquamarine eyes glazing with the sheen of emotional tears. 'I didn't expect you to be faithful.'

'But I *was*,' he asserted levelly.

'And I was too,' she whispered shakily.

'I wouldn't let myself ask you that question.' Gaetano released his breath on an audible hiss. 'But I thank you for making that choice.'

That quickly, Gaetano felt as though he was *all* hers again. There was no ghost of Antonella or any other woman to come between them and make her wonder about comparisons and feel inadequate. Her arms closed round his lean muscular frame, hands smoothing down over his shirt-clad muscular back. 'I can't really convey in words how much that means to me. I made a false assumption. My expectations were too low.'

'I'm far from perfect.'

'I *know*.'

A faint smile tugged at the corners of his shapely mouth. 'You're supposed to tell me I'm perfect, not agree that I'm not.'

'You value honesty,' she reminded him softly, shifting and flexing every muscle to roll him over. 'So, now I shall tell you that you're wearing far too many clothes...'

Lara sat up and embarked on his shirt buttons, plucking them loose, spreading her hands across his bronzed and muscular torso, shimmying down the bed to let her lips follow that same trail. His fingers laced into the tumble of her hair as she ran down his zip and then, without warning, he lifted up again from his prone position and settled her back from him.

'I can't wait,' he groaned. 'I'm like a teenager with you, always frantic to be inside you...'

His frank admission sent a surge of need hurtling through her at storm-force potency and reawakened memories. Gaetano grabbing her in the middle of the day, powered by that simmering passion she couldn't resist, confessing his impatience, apologising, almost embarrassed by the strength of his desire for her and then taking her to orgasmic heaven at record speed.

He was wrenching his jeans down and she helped him, sitting up then too to peel her sundress over her head, laugh as he detached her bra to lift appreciative hands towards her freed breasts and then, with a groan of regret, abandon them to remove the last item

that blocked her body from his. That feverish frantic pace was achingly familiar. In the
midst of it, she kissed him with joy bubbling
up through her.

He flattened her to the pillows with the
power of his response, a hungry growl rip-
pling through his chest as he rearranged her
to his satisfaction. 'I even messed up in bed
with you,' he husked half under his breath.
'You never got the cool version of me.'

'Did you hear me object?'

She angled her hips up to him as he leant
back from her to don protection. She lay back
against the pillows, her body throbbing with
readiness. He entered her fast and deep and
her body jerked at the rush of pure pleasure.
His raw passion, his innate intensity, was one
of the things she loved most about him. He
drove her out of her mind with desire and
broke through her every inhibition with ease.
Excitement climbed as fast as his lethally
effective pace and energy. She reached her
peak equally fast, clenching and convulsing
around him before breaking into a thousand
pieces and floating back to earth, winded and
shaken by the power of the experience.

Gaetano hugged her so tightly without

being prompted to do so that she almost yelped and then he relaxed his hold and released her from his weight while retaining an arm round her to keep her close. Her very bones hummed with contentment.

'The worst thing was not being able to find you,' he admitted abruptly, disconcerting her by raising that particular topic. 'It wasn't until you were gone that I realised how very little you had ever told me about yourself. I knew your father died when you were nine and that you were adopted and that your mother moved around a lot but that was literally it. And it wasn't enough, anywhere near enough, to track you down.'

'My background felt kind of sleazy in comparison to yours.'

'But you didn't know my background when we first met.'

'Your accent, the obvious level of your education, those things gave it away for you and I had my educational years basically stolen from me,' she volunteered ruefully. 'I had a good childhood and great parents until Dad died and then everything I took for granted just disintegrated. Mum couldn't seem to cope without Dad. Every time Mum broke up with her latest man, we had to make a fresh start. And every time I was dragged out of school and put into a new one, which was incredibly disruptive.'

'I had no idea.'

'I was ashamed of it, so I played it down with you.'

'There's plenty of skeletons in my family cupboard.'

'Mum married Alice and Jack's dad and life was stable while she was with him, but she got bored after a year and asked for a divorce,' Lara related uncomfortably, still nervous of sharing that part of her past with him. 'She had a friend in Spain who owned a bar and things only got seriously bad after we moved abroad.'

Gaetano gazed down at her with frowning dark golden eyes. 'Tell me about it...'

'We never had a home of our own. She moved in with her boyfriends and a couple of them took too much interest in me and if I talked to Mum about it, she went crazy with me and accused me of trying to steal them from her. I was only fourteen and more a late starter on the boys front than anything else.'

'*Madonna mia*...how the hell did you cope

with that? That must have been terrifying for you!' Gaetano grated with heat. 'Your adoptive mother was very irresponsible and selfish to subject you to a life of that sort at such a young age.'

'Well, the last guy she was with when I was still there was the worst. He owned his own bar, and I was always helping in the kitchen or clearing tables. I hardly went to school, and it suited them because I was free labour. But when Mum was behind the bar he'd come upstairs and he'd open my bedroom door and stand there staring in and saying, "Just checking on you…" It was the creepiest, scariest thing,' she confessed, drawing in a shallow breath as she shuddered in recollection. 'The way he looked at me, the way he spoke to me, it wasn't right and, eventually, I wrote to my grandparents, Dad's parents, and asked them if I could come home and live with them and go to school. I was lucky they agreed.'

'And what did your mother think of that?'

Lara grimaced. 'I think relief would be the best word to describe her reaction when I told her that I could return to the UK. They even sent me the money for the ticket. Mum couldn't be bothered with me. She was a good mother while Dad was alive, but I think he must have been the one who wanted to adopt the most because once he was gone, she didn't seem to have any real interest in me.'

'I would have understood your situation if you'd confided in me,' Gaetano told her fiercely. 'There was no need to pretty anything up for my benefit.'

'It was more of a matter of personal pride,' she admitted ruefully. 'I didn't want it to seem like there was a huge gulf between us…and then you had to go and turn out to be a prince on the brink of becoming a king. Everything just fell apart then.'

Gaetano wrapped another arm round her. 'That's not going to happen again. It fell apart for both of us that day. We should have had more faith in ourselves and in what we had found with each other.'

She rested her brow down on a smooth brown shoulder and sighed. There was much she could have thrown at him, not least his horrified disbelief when he had realised that he had married her. Only she didn't want to step back into the dangerous ground of the past when the future and the present seemed so much more inviting.

She was on the very edge of a doze when she heard a gong reverberate through the house, the deep boom vibrating through the walls. 'What on earth is that?'

'The dinner warning. Very effective. You can hear it inside and outside,' Gaetano imparted, thrusting back the sheet and lifting her out of bed to settle her barefoot into the biggest, most colourful bathroom she had ever seen.

Twin showers with moulded basins stood side by side. A copper bath was situated beside the window. A huge, tiled vanity with two sinks took up most of the final wall. It was just as Gaetano had said—a house of curiosities—but it was luxurious and full of art and handicrafts.

Dinner was served in the courtyard. Freddy would only pick at his meal. Too many treats, his nanny admitted with a guilty grimace. Lara soothed her concerns, having already noted that the star guest in the Palais des Roses was her son as far as the staff were concerned. They took Freddy out into the beautiful gardens to run around before bedtime. He emerged giggling from under a large shrub and ran to her. She scooped him and his toy rabbit up with an 'oomph' of effort, because he was no lightweight, and cuddled him. He rested his head down drowsily on her shoulder.

'He's getting tired,' she commented.

Gaetano extended his arms and gathered Freddy into them. 'You're a fabulous mother. When I see you with our son, I realise how much I missed out on. He's friendly and very confident because he knows he's loved. I was much more suspicious of new faces and quite lonely,' he admitted as they strolled back towards the house. 'Some day—it doesn't have to be soon—I'd be really happy if you would consider having a second child.'

'Yes,' Lara agreed with a smile. 'I'd like Freddy to have a sibling. I always wanted one myself.'

'At least I had Vittorio.'

'But he was more like a father than a brother. A sibling would be different…someone to play with,' she mused, thinking that Gaetano's big brother had looked like a very serious man in the couple of photos she had seen of him, not the type of parental figure to get into the rough and tumble games that Freddy revelled in.

Gaetano, on the other hand, loved that sort of stuff and didn't object to getting his clothes dirty.

'I'll take him into the pool tomorrow,' Gaetano announced. 'I have a great toddler swimming ring waiting for him. I planned ahead.'

It was a conversation that Lara recalled almost two weeks later as she sat in the shade watching Gaetano entertain their son in the pool. Freddy, safely ensconced in his flamingo ring, chubby little legs kicking, arms waving as he squealed with excitement at his father's antics. Yes, maybe another child was a good idea, Lara thought abstractedly, thinking back with regret of her decision to keep their son a secret on the assumption that their child would be no more welcome to Gaetano than his wife was after he had regained his memory. With hindsight that had been a mistake and perhaps she should have given his recovery from amnesia a few days more before deciding to leave him and their marriage behind her. Only there hadn't been time for her to dally on that decision because Gaetano had been due to fly straight back to Mosvakia.

But Lara didn't want to look back to the past, finding it much more sensible to simply revel in her recent experiences. There had been visits to the souks in the old town of Marrakech. She had bought a pair of soft red leather sliders for Alice, who adored shoes, and a cute wool jacket for Iris. She had even bought a manly leather belt for Alice's brother, Jack, who would be home on leave soon from the army.

And while she was searching for gifts, such as a book on Moroccan history for Dr Beresford, who she remained in contact with, Gaetano had been busy buying gifts for her. There was no stopping him. Anything she liked, Gaetano bought for her. A picture she admired—it became hers. There was a wonderfully shaped and sculpted terracotta urn that would remind her for ever of the colour of the twelfth-century walls surrounding Marrakech when the sun was setting in the early evening.

Nor would she ever forget the vibrant buzz of life and the scent of grilled meat and spices in the air in the Place Jemaa el-Fna. The big square was full of entertainers, dancers, musicians, fortune tellers and snake charmers. Freddy loved snakes, which made his mother shudder. They had toured a lot of public gardens where their son could run free, and their security team could chase after him. They had visited the beach at

Agadir where Freddy had paddled in spite of the breeze, and they had driven out into the countryside where they had seen mule trains carrying goods to market and women balancing tall copper jars of water on their heads.

And there had been some extraordinary moments, she recalled with a dreamy smile. Gaetano had presented her with a spectacular blue diamond ring after dinner in a secluded restaurant in the foothills of the mountains. He knew all the best places to visit, and it had been a magical break but none more magical than the presentation of that ring over mint tea served below the flowering almond trees. He was still trying to talk her out of what he had called her 'cheap' wedding ring and into accepting a new and fancier one, but that ring had too much sentimental value for her to consent to a replacement.

Someone had come to the house to pierce her ears and she was never likely to live down the fact that she had fainted, and that Gaetano had panicked and had insisted on a doctor visiting. Her cheeks could still burn reliving that embarrassing morning. But now she owned a beautiful pair of finely worked traditional earrings that, unfortunately, she would only be able to wear once her ear lobes healed. Gaetano had been disappointed by that news.

Surfacing from her daydream at the sound of her name, she realised that Gaetano needed help with Freddy. Standing up, she grabbed a big towel and went to the edge of the pool to gather the dripping, slippery little body of their toddler into its cosy folds. As she knelt down at the edge, Gaetano left the water as well and followed her across to the sunbed where she had stowed Freddy's clothes.

'My phone rang, and you didn't hear it.' He sighed, drying his hands and grabbing it up.

'Sorry,' Lara muttered as she slotted a wriggling Freddy back into his clothes. 'But answering your phone is a risk and I'm risk-averse, especially after answering it and getting the prime minister!'

'Chicken,' Gaetano taunted with amusement as he punched buttons and walked away with that animal grace that never failed to grab her attention. His bronzed physique spattered with drops of water that sparkled in the sunshine, he still made her tummy turn a somersault and her breath catch in her throat.

She listened to his voice in the distance but tickling Freddy soon drowned Gaetano's conversation out. She moved indoors with her son, looking forward to the cooler evening that would come but decidedly sad that they would be leaving Morocco in the morning. As their nanny reclaimed Freddy, Lara wandered into their bedroom, smiling as she always did when she noticed the spectacular ornate gold metal crown above the big bed from which mosquito netting flowed in a great billowing cascade. Gaetano's grandfather, it seemed, had never forgotten that he was a king even when he was on holiday.

'Something unexpected has come up,' Gaetano said from the doorway. 'Dario is faxing me a copy of the letter addressed to you and he apologises for opening it since it falls into the realm of personal correspondence, but you can blame me for that. He's authorised to open *all* our letters.'

'A letter for me?' Lara frowned. 'But who would write…*personal*?'

'I'll bring the letter for you to read,' Gaetano declared.

'You should get dressed first,' she reminded him.

He glanced down at his swimming trunks and then grimaced, peeling them off in a wet heap to stride into the bathroom.

'Letter?' she queried before he could even turn the water on.

'From a legal firm. Evidently one of Olivier's photos of you was widely taken up and published round the world. A woman in Italy believes that you are the living resemblance of her late British mother and she and her brother are asking if you're willing to take a DNA test to see if you are related to them.'

'Good grief,' Lara gasped, dropping down on the carved chair in the corner with her brain swirling in shock.

'Yes, quite a surprise and your two potential connections are rich and well connected so it's highly unlikely to be any form of a scam. Perhaps you would prefer to look into your birth family for yourself first by your own methods… I don't know. It would take longer but it's up to you.'

Lara blinked rapidly, sheer surprise and bewilderment plunging her into a daze. 'I'll think it over,' was all she could say.

'Don't get your hopes up,' Gaetano advised quietly. 'What are the chances that your parentage could be recognised from a photograph? This will most probably come to nothing.'

CHAPTER NINE

THEY FLEW BACK to Mosvakia very early the following morning. During the flight, Lara could only think about that letter and the truth that if those two people *were* related to her, both her birth parents were dead.

It had been a legal letter, short and to the point, revealing the barest facts but also declaring that the two parties had been looking for their sister, who had been adopted as a newborn, for several years. And although Gaetano had pointed out that the possibility that they could be related to her was a slight one, Lara could only think how wonderful it would be to be so *wanted* and so *important* that people would spend years and presumably a lot of money in search of her. Far too often as she had grown up, she had felt unwanted and tolerated rather than loved. It had often been painful and had contributed to her loneliness and insecurity and possibly even the speed at which she had decided that Gaetano no longer wanted her two years earlier.

'I spent two years searching for you…you didn't give *me* any accolades for it,' Gaetano declared drily.

Lara went pink. 'That was different. I wasn't sure we were legally married, and I assumed you wouldn't want Freddy. But family is a connection I've never had.'

'Except with me and Freddy,' Gaetano informed her with irrefutable logic.

Lara stiffened. 'Until Freddy was born, I had never seen anyone related to me by blood. And Freddy looks exactly like *you*. When I looked up Leah Zanetti online, though, she had black ringlets and I don't look remotely like her or Ari Stefanos.'

Gaetano's shapely mouth curled. 'Don't tear yourself up about this because there's probably nothing in it,' he forecast.

Inexplicably he had realised that he didn't really want Lara to discover long-lost relatives. That would entail sharing her and he wasn't much for sharing any part of her, he acknowledged grudgingly. He quite liked having Lara all to himself. She was the one woman in his entire life who had only ever been his and who focused almost entirely on him. True, he had to share that limelight with Freddy, but he had never enjoyed such closeness in a relationship before. Was he being selfish in not wishing to share Lara? Or was his apprehension more related to the truth that her potential siblings were wealthy enough to provide Lara with an escape hatch should she ever want one from their marriage?

She had walked out on him once. Whether he liked it or not, it could happen again. Lara could be flighty. Hadn't he already learned that? Deep down inside where it was well hidden, Lara had insecurities. She set too low a value on herself. She didn't give her trust easily and she still didn't trust Gaetano. Antonella had only had to hint at a previous relationship with him to cause her very real distress. And in that distress, Lara might have been spooked into leaving him again, Gaetano reasoned worriedly.

Yet he had had to corner her to force her to tell him what was worrying her. Sadly, she had chosen not to trust him with the problem and that problem just created a bigger one. Lara could be vulnerable, and she was very emotional. It was Gaetano's job to protect her and ensure she was happy. But how could he function in that role if she refused to have faith in him?

For possibly the first time he wondered exactly what he had said to Lara the day she walked out on him. In his memory, his recovery from his amnesia, the arrival of Dario and the police and security he had brought with him remained a hopeless blur in which Lara barely featured until she was gone. Only when she had vanished had he appreciated how much of a loss she was to him. So why hadn't he discussed that with her yet? Why, when that one episode was so crucial to the breakdown of their relationship, had he prevented her from even talking about it? Perhaps because even now just remembering that day brought him out in a cold, clammy sweat...

Wondering at Gaetano's unusually quiet mood, Lara accompanied him into Dario's office.

'Have you come to any conclusions?' Dario asked her at the same time as he handed her a glossy magazine folded back to show the relevant page. 'I thought you might want to see the photo that stirred all this up.'

Olivier had sent her digital copies, but Lara wasn't so fond of her image that she had sat down to look at them in any great detail. Now she saw the photo that had attracted Leah Zanetti's interest. It was a close-up and she was smiling, probably laughing at one of Olivier's jokes. She knew from the letter that the other woman believed that she bore a striking resemblance to her late mother, whose newborn baby had been adopted shortly after her death.

'Of course, if the British paps hadn't been so diligently engaged in trying to dig up your background, the fact that you are adopted would never have entered the public domain and it would probably never have occurred to Leah Zanetti that there was a chance that you could be her missing sister,' Gaetano commented. 'Unfortunately, that would make it more difficult for you to check out your birth parentage for yourself because it would be almost impossible to do it discreetly now with the press watching out.'

'Yes,' Lara conceded, wincing because she hadn't thought about that risk, and she was quite sure that her possible siblings wouldn't want that kind of searchlight shed on their family secrets any more than she did.

'The DNA test, however,' Dario imparted as he pulled out a chair for her to sit in, 'would be much more straightforward. It's quick and accurate. You will have an immediate answer, if you're interested.'

'But Lara may *not* be interested in pursuing this further,' Gaetano interposed quietly. 'You once told me that you hadn't enquired into your birth parentage because you were afraid of digging up trouble.'

Her brows pleated at that reminder, and she glanced at his tense profile, wondering why he was so lukewarm, even discouraging, about her researching her background, but before she could speak Dario spoke up for her.

'I don't think that will be an issue. Ari Stefanos has happily acknowledged Leah Zanetti as his half-sister. It seems that his father must have had a long-running affair, which Stefanos only found out about after his father's demise, but nobody would ever have known about that affair if Stefanos hadn't decided to find and acknowledge his sister, Leah,' Dario advanced, his mouth quirking. 'Full marks to him for not caring what anyone said about it.'

Lara had been pondering that warning about press interest, which made her shrink. Now she looked directly at Dario and said, 'I'll agree to the DNA test. It seems the easiest option.'

'Are you sure you've thought it through?' Gaetano prompted.

'Yes, I'd rather know one way or the other, even if it means I'm disappointed.' Lara raised her head high. 'They're both married with children. Do you realise that that could mean that *I* have nieces and nephews?' she murmured in wonderment. 'A sister and a half-brother? It's so exciting!'

'I'll make the arrangements for the test,' Dario announced. 'It can be done today and sent off.'

'Don't forget that this may only be a mirage,' Gaetano breathed, closing an arm round her slender back to guide her out of the office again.

'Why are you so down on me looking into this?' Lara demanded of him in the corridor.

'I'm not down on it. I just don't want you to get hurt,' Gaetano parried, casting a tense look down at her delicate freckled profile. 'You're already investing too much in what may be false hopes.'

Lara spun and tiptoed her fingers down over his lean, muscular midriff in reproach. 'You're such a gloomster sometimes.'

His hand captured her wandering digits. 'I'm more realistic than you, *bambola*. Let's discuss something more practical...perhaps, the party we're holding next week to introduce you to everyone?'

Lara paled. 'You didn't warn me about that.'

'I'm proud of you and I want to show you off. Do you remember that gorgeous ball gown you insisted that you'd never ever wear? It's for this party. I've already organised travel for Alice to attend and I promise I won't leave your side for a moment,' he intoned huskily. 'I'll act as though we're chained together.'

'And then everyone will say, "Look at how trapped he looks with her!"' Lara quipped with amusement.

He gazed down at her, dark golden eyes full of heat and hunger. 'Or, look how much he *enjoys* being trapped with her?'

The DNA test was quickly carried out that same morning. Conscious of Gaetano's warnings, Lara put the whole matter to the back of her mind because she didn't want to build fantasy castles in the air. Shortly before lunch, Gaetano appeared with an air of purpose etched into his lean dark features and walked

her into the dining room. With the wine poured
and the meal awaiting them, he dismissed the
server and tucked her into a seat.

'Where's Dario?'

'He went home to Carla for lunch and plans
to return to that arrangement. Vittorio didn't
like staff leaving the palace to eat. He made a
lot of rules and I'm changing some of them.'

Lara sipped her wine.

'Now…' Gaetano hesitated, his mouth tightening. 'Something I've been avoiding but which
was a major experience for both of us. I'd like
to talk about the day I regained my memory.'

Lara glanced at him in surprise. 'I thought
that was on the forbidden list.'

'That wasn't one of my wisest decisions,'
Gaetano admitted tautly. 'As I've already admitted, I don't remember that day's events
very well. I saw Dario on that path and immediately recognised him. But when my two
worlds—the one with you and the one I originally came from—merged all of a sudden…
everything blurred. I got lost between the past
and the present.'

Time had already slid back for Lara to that
momentous day. She was staring into mid-air
while recalling how on edge she had been

even before the helicopters landed. 'Cathy's son, Patrick came home unexpectedly the night before his mother had texted to tell me that he'd lost his job and was coming back home for a while—'

'I remember Jamie and how drunk he was when his friend dropped him off.'

'You helped me put him to bed. I was fretting about how much longer we could stay with Patrick in residence. With him there to take care of the pets and everything, we were surplus. And I didn't know where we were going to go at short notice or how we would live when we got there,' she completed weakly.

'We'd only finished breakfast when the helicopters landed in the field on the other side of the road,' Gaetano recalled.

Lara remembered racing upstairs to have a better view of what was happening and when she had seen all those men converging on the farmhouse, some of them clearly policemen, she had started to panic. They had traced Gaetano by a sighting from a local in a neighbouring village. Rushing back downstairs, she had joined Gaetano at the front door as a young, bearded man wearing a troubled expression had come through the gate.

Gaetano's arm had dropped from her shoulders, and he had said slowly, heavily, almost as though he had been drugged, 'Dario... what's happened?'

And the two men had stood there chattering volubly in Italian while she'd hovered like a third wheel, desperate to know what was going on but shut out by the language barrier. It was Dario who had guided Gaetano back indoors and urged him down into a seat. For the first time, Gaetano had recognised someone, and it was obvious that with that recognition his memory had returned just as quickly as he had lost it. Whatever he had learned from Dario had left him looking drawn and devastated. Finally, she had tugged at his sleeve to remind him of her presence.

'Dario, this is my wife, Lara...use English, please.'

'Your *wife*, Your Majesty?' Dario had been stunned almost speechless by that introduction.

'Don't call me that,' Gaetano had urged sickly.

'What else can I call you? You became our King the instant your brother died,' Dario had proclaimed.

'That was the moment,' Gaetano murmured, dragging Lara back to the present after that mutual surge of recollection. 'That was the moment when I realised what a hash I'd made of everything.'

'In marrying me,' Lara completed tightly, pale as milk and pushing her plate away.

'No, in leaving home without my phone, in going off grid and the way I'd married you in *secret*. I was in shock at Vittorio's death and the knowledge that I had to step up to the throne. My brother was terminally ill. That's why he sent me away. He said he wouldn't have me hovering by his deathbed like Giulia and that I had to enjoy what freedom I had left before I was forced to replace him. But he believed he had months of life left,' Gaetano advanced.

'Just before you explained our marriage in Italian to Dario, you looked at me in horror and said, "What the hell have I done?"' Lara swallowed hard and pushed back from the table to rise and move over to the windows. She folded her arms because her hands were shaking. 'And it seemed quite clear to me that the minute that you realised *who* you were, you regretted marrying me.'

'That's not how it was,' Gaetano countered in fierce disagreement. 'I was in a state of disbelief that I had married *anyone*! Lara, I was a hopeless womaniser before I met you and I'd never had a normal relationship with a woman! I had never been in love either. I had sex. I had a lot of sex but not with anyone who mattered to me. You were in a class of your own and I was blown away that I had met you, fallen in love with you and married you that quickly.'

Lara swallowed hard. 'Well, I interpreted your attitude differently. I assumed that you deeply regretted our marriage and Dario's re-action convinced me that you thought you'd made a mistake in marrying me.'

His ebony brows pleated. 'That's not how I felt. But I can see now that I was being selfish that day and only focusing on my own concerns. I was totally blind to how you might be reacting to the news that you had married a royal and… I think *you* panicked.'

Lara breathed in deep and slow to calm herself, ready to snap back at that reading of her behaviour. But she connected with brilliant dark golden eyes fringed by lush black lashes and lifted her chin, unable to lie to him. 'Yes, you're right. Later I couldn't admit that to myself—that I had panicked. But you had also made me feel rejected… I felt I wasn't good enough to be married to you. Add in that I genuinely believed that our marriage might be illegal then and I had no good reason to stay.'

'*I* should have been your reason to stay,' Gaetano told her, setting his empty wine glass down with a snap as he stood up. 'I relied on you. I trusted you. You are the first woman I ever trusted apart from Giulia and yet you walked out on me when I needed you the most!'

Lara was badly shaken by that condemnation. 'You *needed* me?' she whispered.

'Of course, I did when I'd just lost the only family I had. I was grieving for my brother. I had the throne, but I didn't want it... I had never wanted it. I was closer to you than I'd ever been to anyone and when you disappeared, it almost destroyed me. I went through the year that followed like a zombie on autopilot. I wasn't expecting you to walk out on me and disappear. I wasn't prepared for that to happen...and I *still* have this ridiculous fear that you will vanish again!' Gaetano ground out in a raw undertone.

Tears of guilt and discomfiture were lashing Lara's eyes. She closed the distance between them and wrapped her arms tightly round him, gripped by a powerful wave of remorse. 'If I had understood that you needed me, I would never have left you.'

'But you did, and you can't turn back time and change it. It happened. You had your reasons for doubting my commitment to you. I neglected to give you the reassurance you needed, and I have to learn to live with that,' he breathed tautly.

'I had to live without you too,' Lara whispered shakily.

'But you *chose* to do that… I didn't. And I missed out on Freddy as a baby.'

'I can't change those things,' Lara pointed out wretchedly as her arms dropped from him.

'I know.' Gaetano bent his handsome dark head and claimed her lips with a hungry sound of urgency before she could step back from him. 'I'm working on myself,' he declared against her swollen mouth, returning for another taste with intense enthusiasm.

Three days later, Dario entered the nursery to find Lara reading Freddy his favourite storybook complete with all the choo-choo noises that accompanied it and made her son squeal with laughter. He held out an envelope. 'This came marked urgent. I guessed what it was and thought you'd like some privacy to open it.'

Lara smiled at him, marvelling at the change that had occurred in their relationship. The longer she had known him, the friendlier and warmer Gaetano's right-hand man had become. She had begun to admire his efficiency, his fierce loyalty to Gaetano and his protectiveness towards him. She understood exactly what had caused his more aggressive attitude the first time they had met. His driving motivation was always Gaetano's wellbeing and if Gaetano had got himself into the wrong marriage, Dario would have been the first to help him to get out of it again.

Lara left her son to his nap and wandered off to the sitting room to open the letter. It had to be the DNA results. She tore it open and lifted out the paper within. A little scream of excitement broke from her parted lips. She had a sister, an actual living, breathing sister, which meant that she had a half-brother as well, not to mention a whole host of nieces and nephews! She performed a little happy dance in the middle of the room. She would finally be able to find out the whole story of who she was and where she came from and she could discover it all in private from the brother and sister who had been involved in that same story. She thought that would be wonderful.

She looked for Gaetano and couldn't find him. She headed for Dario's office, hoping he would be able to help her find her sister's email address or phone number, so that she could make the next move. She heard male voices within and hovered, reluctant to walk in on an official meeting of some kind. She smiled as she heard Gaetano speak, his deep dark voice louder than usual.

'I ignored all your advice and it's come back to bite me. I believed I was deceiving Lara! That was the price of getting them *both* home to Mosvakia. I had to make her believe that it was a reconciliation. I couldn't face a court battle for custody or doing anything more underhand, like luring her out here and then springing a custody suit on her in a Mosvakian court. And all the time I believed that we were happy because I was a great actor, I was *lying* to myself…in fact I was lying to myself from the very minute I met her again!'

'You have to be the only person in the palace unaware of that piece of self-deception.' Dario chuckled. 'In this one field alone, you have no game. I caught on to the true story before we even left England.'

Lara blinked, emerging from her daze, anguish clawing at her, destroying her happiness, her confidence, her calm. She couldn't breathe. It was as if someone had cut off her oxygen supply. She stumbled away, in search of a little dark hole to hide in. She had been so stupid, she had been so dreadfully stupid to trust him, particularly where Freddy was concerned.

It was obvious that Freddy, rather than Freddy's mother, had been Gaetano's most desired acquisition. He had wanted custody of his son and the easiest way to accomplish that goal had been to persuade Lara that he wanted a reconciliation. Well, he had got what he wanted. Could it be said that he was simply making the best of a bad job where their marriage was concerned? Since he was stuck with her anyway, he was suggesting they consider having another child. But why had he also said that he was afraid of her vanishing again?

Where's your wits, Lara? Of course, Gaetano would be afraid of that development because he knew that if she left, she would be taking his son with her. And there was no deception there, was there? Gaetano indisputably adored his son and enjoyed being a father. He took breaks in the busiest day to spend time with Freddy. And their son was equally attached to his father. Freddy was benefiting from having two parents in a stable relationship. So, an immediate desire to run and keep on running from Gaetano would be a bad, selfish idea, she acknowledged.

She walked into their bedroom, still struggling to catch her breath as she hung onto the door handle for support. She had believed what she wanted to believe: that Gaetano had genuinely missed her and wanted her back. It had been too good to be true, but she hadn't smelled a rat, had she? No, she had jumped back into his arms faster than the speed of light.

When had she forgotten that the guy she loved had been a notorious womaniser before their marriage? A man with loads of experience, practised at persuading women to believe what he wanted them to believe? So, he had given her the fairy story and she had swallowed it whole.

But this time he wasn't going to get away with chewing her up and spitting her out, she thought bitterly. This time, there would be a reckoning…

CHAPTER TEN

GAETANO FINALLY FOUND Lara lying fast asleep on their bed. He had looked everywhere else for her. The staff had been looking too. Her phone had been found in the nursery.

He had expected her to approach him once she'd received the news of the positive DNA test but she had kept her distance. Gaetano, on the other hand, hadn't had that luxury with her siblings. Ari Stefanos had phoned first and, assuming that Gaetano was already aware of that positive test, had asked when he could speak to his newly found sister because he wanted to arrange a visit to Mosvakia as soon as possible. Leah Zanetti had rung next, bubbling with excitement and enthusiasm, every bit as eager to meet Lara.

Gaetano had told them both that they were very welcome to visit and stay at the palace and was only a little taken aback when they announced that they would be arriving the following day. Presumably, Lara would be ecstatic because she would have them with her at the party.

Gaetano stared down at his slumbering wife. Sadly, Lara didn't look ecstatic about the discovery that she had a new family. Weren't those tear stains on her cheeks? Maybe it was just the emotional charge of that new knowledge that had stressed her out and saddened her. He was also wondering how she would handle the rather forceful personalities he had recognised on the phone. Lara was quiet, gentle and vulnerable and even if she decided that she didn't much like Ari and Leah, she would pretend otherwise because she was kind and always thinking about other people's feelings. They had better not hurt or disappoint her, Gaetano thought grimly, *or* try to interfere in their marriage.

'Yes, I appreciate that you've been married for two years but you didn't announce the marriage,' Ari Stefanos had reminded Gaetano sardonically on the phone. 'And from what I understand my sister was on her own raising your child for those two years. Of course I've got questions.'

So, no, Gaetano wasn't looking forward to meeting Lara's brother and sister quite as much as he might have been. He did not think that his past misunderstandings with Lara were anyone's business but their own.

Lara came awake slowly and for a moment she drifted until her brain kicked back into gear and then she sat up with a start, thoroughly disconcerted to see Gaetano working on his laptop at the table in the corner of the room. Pushing her tumbled hair off her brow, she mumbled, 'Why are you working in here?'

'I wanted to be here when you woke up. I was worried about you. I thought you'd come to tell me about the positive DNA test but you didn't.'

'I fell asleep…not enough sleep last night,' she framed, her cheeks warming, but for once she didn't try to meet his liquid dark golden gaze with the understanding mutual glow of a couple who were unable to keep their hands off each other for very long.

'My fault. Your brother and your sister will be flying in tomorrow.'

'Tomorrow?' she prompted in shock.

'They're exceptionally keen to meet you.

Both of them phoned but we couldn't track you down. You left your phone in the nursery,' he reminded her.

Lara groaned and breathed in slow and deep. Her plan to stage an immediate showdown with Gaetano was now impossible. She didn't want to stage a show of a troubled marriage for her new brother and sister. And naturally that would be a consequence of her tackling Gaetano head-on now about the fake reconciliation tactics he had used on her. There would be a huge row. And after that, there would be no hope of hiding the tension and awkwardness between them. So, for the present, she had to hold her fire.

From below her feathery lashes, she studied him. In the well-tailored charcoal-grey suit that outlined his lithe, powerful physique, he was breathtakingly good-looking. Black hair, stunning dark deep-set eyes, perfect bone structure. And on the surface, he was so courteous, considerate and supportive, but that could only be a smooth, sophisticated façade hiding the real truth of his feelings. Deep down inside he had to resent her for being so necessary to Freddy that she and her son were a package deal.

It was cold consolation that he had never said he loved her, but then she hadn't said those words either. At least he hadn't uttered that lie. It hardly mattered when Gaetano had sucked her in and spat her out, shredding her heart all over again. What was it about him that got to her every time? No matter what he did, no matter how he behaved? She couldn't allow love to make a fool of her again. There had to be honesty without lies or pretty pretences.

'I thought you'd be more excited about your brother and sister.'

'I am, maybe just a little nervous. Are they bringing their families?'

'They didn't say. And we've plenty of space if they do but I would suspect they'll only bring their partners. I warned them about the party tomorrow night and told them that they're very welcome to join us,' he completed quietly.

As usual he had thought of everything. Her chest felt tight, her throat even tighter. She needed to get a grip on herself again, she told herself angrily. She needed to be the best actor she could be for the next day or so, at least until her siblings had departed again and she had the privacy to confront Gaetano. And what was she going to tell him?

Yes, what was she planning to call him out on? How dare you give me my dream marriage? How dare you make me happy? How dare you convince me that what we have is real when it's *not*? In truth, he might have lied but he had lived up to every one of his promises.

'You don't seem happy. You're not reacting the way I expected.' Gaetano rose with feral grace and dropped down on the side of the bed to curve an arm round her. 'What's worrying you? Are you afraid that they won't like you? Don't be daft. You're a lovely person and they'll see that in you, just as other people do.'

'Gaetano—' she said in embarrassment.

'You know, I used to be the kingpin around here, but I'm afraid Freddy outshines both of us. However, we've got a chef who wants to know how to fatten you up and I told him that there was no chance of doing that. And Dario wants to serve you up first to the Spanish ambassador because you speak Spanish.'

'Only some. Four years in Spain,' she reminded him unnecessarily.

'Your siblings will absolutely love you,' Gaetano asserted with confidence.

Lara felt as if her heart were cracking inside her, as if he had just put a hand inside her chest and squeezed it, because she loved him and almost every time he spoke he reminded her *why* she loved him. How could she still be feeling like that after what she had overheard?

Leah and Gio Zanetti and Ari Stefanos and his wife, Cleo, all flew in on the same flight and arrived at the palace together. Alice had been upset that she was unable to attend the party because an aunt had died suddenly, and she was driving up north to visit the family.

Lara was very nervous, but she need not have been because her sister, Leah, chattered away freely, releasing her from tongue-tied reticence. It was Leah's older brother, Ari, who told Leah to slow down before she frightened Lara off. Leah kept on staring at her and then apologised, digging into her capacious bag to pull out a small photo album. 'This is all I've got, I'm afraid. I went through several foster homes, and I lost stuff. But this is Mum and, although she's older than you here, you can see how much you resemble her and why I was totally knocked back when I saw that picture of you in the magazine.'

Lara stared down at the image and she too recognised the strong similarity in colouring and facial shape.

'You've got her eyes, absolutely her eyes!' Leah carolled. 'They're a very unusual shade.'

'Aquamarine,' Gaetano slotted in. 'The very first thing I noticed about Lara was her eyes.'

'Who's the little boy with you?' Lara asked her sister as she studied the photos.

And Leah told her about her twin brother, Lucas, who had died from an overdose. Lara's eyes swam with tears, and she sniffed, only beginning to regain her composure when Ari told her that Lucas and his girlfriend had left behind a baby, whom he and Cleo had adopted, a little girl they called Lucy.

'My goodness, there's so much I have to catch up on,' Lara exclaimed. 'But that was a wonderful conclusion to a sad story.'

'Twins run through the family. Ari was a twin. We have twins and Ari has a set too,' Leah told her. 'You've been warned.'

It wasn't very long before the three siblings were catching up on family history.

'Now I want to know how on earth you met and married a king!' Leah announced as Lara poured her fresh coffee.

'And why it took two years for Gaetano to bring you and your son back to the palace,' Ari completed more seriously, taking a seat beside Lara.

For the first time, Lara felt comfortable enough to tell other people that story with all its twists and turns and misunderstandings.

'Clearly you love him and if he makes you happy, I'm happy for you, but if you have any doubts, I hope you know that you can always come to Leah or me for support,' Ari completed before going on to tell her about her inheritance from her late father and a few more facts about the paternal half of her background.

Leah was more interested in finding out about Lara's life after the adoption and that took some time to cover and both women got quite emotional during the discussion.

'Mum would never ever have given you up if she'd lived and it would have broken her heart if she'd known what happened to you afterwards. I can't believe that you're not even still in contact with your adoptive mother.'

'She had no wish to stay in touch. I'm not part of her life any more. I'm used to it now.' A rueful smile lit Lara's face as Leah squeezed her shoulder in comfort.

'I want you to come to Italy and stay with us so that I can really get to know you. I've been longing to find my little sister ever since I lost her,' Leah told her evocatively. 'I held you in my arms and helped to feed you when you were only a few days old. But I never expected to find you living in a palace.'

'And I never expected to marry a royal! I'd love to come to Italy and stay with you,' Lara declared as she stood up. 'Now come and meet Freddy. I can't wait to meet your children.'

'I'd love you to visit Cleo and me in Greece as well,' Ari confided quietly.

Gaetano hovered, his lean, darkly handsome features taut and serious. 'I have a business meeting I can't cancel,' he said apologetically. 'But I'll see you all at lunch.'

Lunch went well. Leah opted to join Lara when the beauty stylist, organised for her, arrived to do her nails and hair and immediately called in back-up to look after Leah as well. Lara was more than ready for a little personal grooming help in advance of the party that evening. The number of confidences that her siblings had made had helped Lara to keep her mind busy and her spirits up, but once Leah left her to return to her room that overheard conversation between Gaetano and Dario returned to haunt Lara and it hit her mood hard.

Gaetano had only chosen to be with her for Freddy's sake. She remembered him telling her that his brother's marriage to Giulia had been one of convenience. Possibly that was one reason why he was willing to accept a similar arrangement for himself. But he *had* to feel that he was settling for less than he deserved. Freddy might benefit from having his mother, but Gaetano would be losing out in the personal stakes.

The more she thought about her situation, the angrier Lara became. Lara didn't care how good his intentions might have been. Gaetano hadn't given her a choice about what *she* wanted and needed. What she had learned had made her feel...*less*, decimating her pride and her confidence. She didn't want to be any man's second-best or convenient bride. She didn't want to be merely tolerated because she was Freddy's mother. She wanted to be loved, madly lusted after, *valued*. She didn't want to be the one who loved and lusted alone, always the bridesmaid, never the bride.

Clad in a pretty lingerie set from her new collection, Lara was tweaking her make-up in the en suite bathroom when Gaetano entered the bedroom to get changed. He paused in the doorway, shooting Lara an appreciative scrutiny. Her high full breasts artfully cradled in a strapless pale blue lace bra matched with bikini knickers made him release a low whistle. 'You look incredibly sexy in that get-up.'

Lara whirled round to face him. 'You deceived me!' she heard herself condemn out of hand, inwardly wincing but unable to suppress the angry swell pushing up inside her when she saw him. 'You let me think we were having a real reconciliation when all the time it was just a big fat *empty* fraud!'

Taken aback by that attack, Gaetano stared back at her with stunned intensity. 'Back up a minute…where is this coming from?'

'I heard you talking to Dario in your office.'

His brows pleated. 'Dario hasn't been in my office since yesterday.'

'*So?*' Lara interrupted aggressively, brows raised, mouth compressed. 'You think you're the only one around here who can pride themselves on their acting ability?'

'You mean you've been sitting on these crazy assumptions of yours since *yesterday*?' Gaetano demanded incredulously. 'All these nasty suspicions were going on below the surface and I had no blasted idea?'

The thundering annoyance in his raised voice only provoked a shrug of Lara's slight shoulder. 'Not so nice, is it, when you're not the one in the know?' she quipped.

'Are you aware of that saying that eavesdroppers never hear good of themselves?' Gaetano asked grimly as he slid free of his jacket and yanked loose his tie to toss them back into the bedroom.

'Well, I heard the truth.'

'If you'd stayed long enough to hear the truth, you wouldn't be attacking me now!' Gaetano blitzed back with unhidden annoyance. 'And as you didn't stay, you didn't hear the whole conversation and went away with completely the *wrong* impression of what I was talking about.'

Lara shrugged another shoulder, her face

tense. 'Of course, you're going to say something like that in circumstances like this. You want to put a lid on this argument before the party. You're going to make some very smooth and practised explanation and try to hang me out to dry and convince me that I didn't hear what I heard. I know how you operate.'

'There are some definite markers requiring further exploration in that speech, *bambola*—'

'Don't call me that now as if you're fond of me!' Lara practically spat at him in her rage. What was infuriating her most was that the angrier she became, the cooler and calmer Gaetano seemed to be.

'You don't think that I could possibly *be* fond of you? *Dio mio.* Evidently, no matter how smooth and practised you believe me to be, I seem to have failed utterly to impress you with my ability to be truthful and sincere.'

'Ha!' Lara snapped, unimpressed, as she pushed past him to return to the bedroom, stalking in her high heels. 'Back in England, you tied me into knots with your cleverly chosen words and I believed you every step of the way…so much for that!'

'And so much for your perception and self-belief,' Gaetano traded with sardonic clarity.

Hands on hips, Lara spun back to him. 'What's that supposed to mean? You implied that you regretted our marriage breakdown and that you wanted us to be a couple again.'

'As far as it goes, that was true. I knew that I had to bring Freddy back to Mosvakia and I didn't want to fight you through the courts for custody of him. I was determined not to frighten or intimidate you with threats of legal action.'

'I could have coped!' Lara slung back at him with determination.

'You didn't deserve that. You're a brilliant mother but Freddy is the heir to the throne, and I couldn't leave him with you in the UK. He needs to grow up here and learn about who he is. That's my duty: to do what's best for the Crown, regardless of how fair or unfair it is,' Gaetano breathed in a raw undertone. 'Freddy belongs with you *and* me and you belong with me as well. We're together. We're a family. No way was I prepared to fight you in court and threaten to take him away from you. He needs you every bit as much as he needs me.'

'So you lied to me by letting me believe that it was *me* you wanted back more than Freddy because you guessed that that would be a winning proposal.'

'Yes,' Gaetano conceded with none of her drama. 'But lying is a harsh description of what I did to get you both back.'

'Sorry if I offended!'

'I had no idea what my feelings for you were at the time,' Gaetano disconcerted her by admitting. 'I knew that I was still hugely attracted to you the instant I saw you again, but I was still at war with what happened when we fell in love two years ago.'

'At war?' she queried with a frown of in-comprehension.

'You caused that war, Lara,' Gaetano told her. 'When you walked out and disappeared on me, I couldn't believe or accept that we *had* loved each other. People who love each other don't usually lose faith in each other that suddenly.'

Lara lost colour. 'I don't know what you're talking about.'

'Yes, you do. You just don't want to hear it,'

Gaetano incised gravely. 'When you walked out, it made me doubt my feelings for you. The way I saw it, if you could walk away that easily you had never had true feelings for me. That fast I told myself that I'd never been in love with you even to begin with.'

'Two years ago I thought you regretted our marriage. I thought leaving and disappearing was the kindest thing I could do!' Lara shot back at him shakily, all her emotions swelling inside her tight chest.

'That may be true but that's not how it affected me. It wrecked me *and* the trust I had in you. Don't tell me that I didn't feel what I felt,' Gaetano warned her very seriously. 'You're not the only one of us who got badly hurt.'

Lara was trembling and thinking that wasn't it just typical that she confronted Gaetano and all of a sudden he was turning everything round and blaming her for walking out on him in the first place.

'Do you know how I managed without you? I told myself that I hadn't really loved you and that it was an infatuation. Back then, I didn't think I had it in me to fall in love as deeply and as fast as I did with you. So, naturally, it had to be an illusion.'

'I thought stuff like that too,' Lara confessed reluctantly.

'But I was wrong,' Gaetano declared. 'I really do wish you'd heard that whole conversation I had with Dario.'

Lara grimaced. 'I didn't want to listen to you laughing at me.'

'No, the laugh was entirely on me. I was finally admitting that I was as much in love with you as ever and Dario was the one laughing. He pointed out that everyone else in the palace had guessed how I felt about you *weeks* ago,' he confided.

Her aquamarine eyes had widened. 'In love with me?' she echoed blankly.

'You didn't guess?' Gaetano asked in surprise. 'I mean, Dario said I was about as subtle as a thunderstorm. He said I changed so fast from wanting a divorce to announcing our reconciliation that his head was left spinning. He worked out what was happening to me ages before I understood my own feelings.'

'Did he?' Lara whispered, still up in the air

without a parachute and barely able to credit what Gaetano was telling her.

'I used Freddy and my desire not to engage in a court battle over him as an excuse to get you back. That approach was a sop to my pride. I wasn't ready to admit how I still felt about you.' Gaetano winced. 'I think I was even a bit scared to put myself out there with you again—'

Tears erupted from Lara's eyes, and she dashed them away with a trembling hand. Could she have been so stupid that she didn't recognise how he felt about her? She remembered Morocco, which had been one long, wonderful, magical honeymoon full of romance and tenderness and passion. She was in shock and yet when she looked back at the amount of daily attention and support he gave her, she was rocked by her own inability to acknowledge the love that he had shown her.

'And I'm still absolutely terrified of losing you again,' Gaetano breathed grimly.

'I need to apologise to you for not having faith in you and for not trusting my own judgement,' Lara whispered unevenly. 'I've suffered a lot of rejection in life from people I cared about, and I think I was much too quick to assume that you were rejecting me two years ago. That's sad because it means we lost out on each other, and you lost out on knowing Freddy from the beginning. But whether you find it hard to believe or not, I have always loved you…practically from the first moment I saw you and right up until now when you've got the courage to share how *you* feel.'

'And make you cry,' Gaetano pointed out ruefully. 'You're not just saying that you love me because you think that's what I need to hear?'

'Don't be silly,' Lara urged as she unbuttoned his shirt, and he took the hint and toed off his shoes. 'I love you to death and back.'

'And even last night when you thought I had deceived you, you *still*—'

Lara turned beet red. 'A good memory on that score is not always appreciated. I'm not very good at saying no to you.'

'Long may it last,' Gaetano husked with fervent appreciation and he lifted her to lay her down on the bed.

'You said you don't believe in it, but it was kind of love at first sight, wasn't it?' Lara prompted on the back of a blissful sigh and then she sat up with a start. 'The party! We can't do this now!'

Gaetano's lips claimed hers with scorching hunger and her spine liquefied, heat arrowing down into her pelvis. He followed her down onto the bed. He told her that he loved her again and she reciprocated with enthusiasm as he made her his again. It was fast and wildly passionate. In the aftermath of immense pleasure, her body feeling pleasantly floaty, she belatedly recalled the party and almost fell out of bed in her haste to get dressed. Gaetano was already out of the shower, and she raced in.

Arrayed in a fresh set of lacy lingerie, she lifted her ball gown. It ranged from a purple shade at the neck and slowly deepened down into the richest violet. Crystals were scattered across the full skirt and narrow diamanté straps crossed her shoulders catching the light. It was a dream of a dress, she thought happily as she eased her feet into her high heels.

'Let me help you with the jewellery,' Gaetano urged, flipping open the boxes stacked in readiness on the dresser and extracting a sapphire necklace to clasp it around her slender throat. 'You look utterly amazing, *bambola mia*.'

Lara donned the sapphire and diamond drop earrings and smiled at him, exhilaration brightening her eyes and lifting the curve of her lips. 'For the first time ever I feel amazing,' she told him honestly. 'I'm afraid we're late.'

'The main guests should make an entrance,' Gaetano teased.

'I love you,' she told him in the lift, a new confidence in her upright carriage.

'I love you even more,' he whispered as they stepped out into the glittering gathering of guests in the palace foyer, smiles on their faces, immense warmth in their hearts and contentment in their eyes.

EPILOGUE

Seven years later

LARA THOUGHT BACK to that wonderful party with Leah and Ari by her side, her brother and sister, who had been so proud to acknowledge their relationship, and she smiled. There had been many parties since then. Christmases, birthdays, christenings and holidays in the UK, Italy, Greece, Morocco and Mosvakia. Internationally based family members made for a lot of travel. And then there were the shopping trips she enjoyed with Leah and Cleo. The Christmas shopping trips were especially enjoyable.

'Why did you once tell me that you didn't like Christmas?' she had asked Gaetano a couple of years earlier as he'd helped her decorate one of the many festive trees in their wing of the palace.

'When I was a child, Vittorio only attended official celebrations and they were boring. By the time I got to eighteen, Christmas was just an endless string of exhausting parties. And *then*,' he had stressed, turning to look down at her possessively, 'I saw you in front of a Christmas tree and fell madly in love and that sort of jolted me out of my dislike of the season. It made Christmas a whole new occasion to appreciate. And then you gave me Freddy and the rest of our little tribe, and I realised Christmas is all about children having fun. I never had that, but I want our children to have it.'

It was their turn to stage the family Christmas this year and the palace was already hopping with children having a whale of a time. Freddy had discovered that his older cousin, Lucy, wasn't impressed when he announced that he was a prince and that he should be in charge even though he was younger. Gaetano had told his son that he should be looking out for his siblings, five-year-old Rosa and three-year-old Tommaso. Freddy had heaved a sigh of disgust, protesting that Tommaso was still a baby who ate with his fingers if he could get away with it, while Rosa insisted on lugging a baby doll and buggy everywhere.

Leah and Gio had three boys and two girls and Ari and Cleo had four boys and a girl, so the games they played could be fairly rough and lively, even with supervision. As far as Lara was concerned their own family was complete but Gaetano was trying to persuade her to consider one more pregnancy. She had said she would think about it while pointing out that they had so far contrived to miss out on a twin arrival, and it might not be wise to tempt providence. Gaetano, however, was very much of the 'more the merrier' persuasion and was willing to take that risk.

Life was good but frantically busy. Lara now had a busy social life. And as her confidence grew, she had ventured out from behind closed doors in the palace to take on a children's charity. Other responsibilities and requests for her presence had quickly followed. She had spread her wings a little but still zealously guarded her time with Gaetano and her children. Time went by so fast, and she didn't want to miss out on the children's early years.

Gaetano joined her in the once formal

drawing room, which had all the space they needed to entertain her relatives and friends. Alice was joining them with her husband, Rory, Iris and her little boy, Amos. Dario and Carla, along with their baby, Sofia, would also be part of the festivities.

'You seem thoughtful,' Lara remarked as Gaetano studied her, his dark golden gaze brilliant below the thick canopy of his lashes.

'You look good,' he told her, scanning the short velvet fitted skirt she had teamed with a soft silk shirt, her shapely legs crossed and capped by slender high heels.

It was Christmas Eve and their wedding anniversary, and later, they would be having a special dinner with their family and friends and attending a carol service at midnight. The most beautiful tree took up the whole of one corner. It was the family tree, the one adorned with the children's hand-crafted gifts and ornaments that had been bought to commemorate certain events. Decorating it was an annual exercise of reliving fond memories.

'It scares me to think that I might never have met you,' Gaetano admitted, startling her. 'That bout of amnesia was the best thing that ever happened to me.'

Her aquamarine eyes widened in surprise. 'How can you say that?'

'I didn't know who I was, and the amnesia allowed the *real* me to emerge…the guy I would have been had I not been born royal and conditioned to be a cold bastard,' he breathed through compressed lips. 'Vittorio did his best with me, but I was taught to suppress every normal emotion.'

'I know, but he was too buttoned up himself to see any other way of handling your temperament,' she told him gently, knowing how guilty he felt if he criticised his late brother.

'I didn't let loose until I met you and the instant I was free of those fetters, what did I do? I fell in love and married you within days and then, when I regained my memory, I thought that I must have been insane to do something like that. But in reality, I was doing what came naturally to me.'

'Only it shocked the life out of you when you recovered your memory and found a wedding ring on your finger,' Lara reminded him.

He stretched out a hand to her. 'Come here…' he urged and as she crossed the room he caught her hand in his and slid a glittering ring onto her finger. 'An eternity ring for our anniversary. Sapphires and emeralds to match your eyes, *bambola*.'

Her eyes shone. 'It's beautiful, Gaetano.'

'I was telling you the truth when I told you that I didn't have a single happy moment without you. I was re-energised the minute I saw you again, although I did try to play it cool,' he murmured with husky amusement. 'You transformed my life, and you gave me the strength to be the man I am now.'

When he looked at her in a certain way, her whole body lit up like a traffic light and pulsed with sexual energy. 'I love you…'

Gaetano reached down to grasp her waist and hoisted her up against him. 'And I'm about to take advantage.'

'We *can't*!' Lara gasped. 'Our guests?'

Gaetano grinned down at her as he elbowed his way out of the room, taking the shortcut down a former servant's staircase to their bedroom. 'Already organised. Our guests are taking the kids to the Winter Fair to give us some downtime to celebrate our anniversary,' he imparted.

'You don't do that to your guests!' Lara moaned in horror.

'They're family and they understand that we can't help the fact that our anniversary is Christmas Eve and we're usually entertaining or in someone else's house. And thank you for making your family my family as well. Sometimes they come in very useful!' he teased.

Lara punched his shoulder in mock rebuke as he dropped her down on the bed and slipped off her heels, following her down to claim her mouth passionately with his own. Clothes fell away like confetti in a breeze. There was passion and laughter and joy and great tenderness. As usual, Gaetano's sheer intensity blew her away and, in the aftermath, she felt buoyant with happiness.

'I'm insanely in love with you,' he groaned into her tumbled hair, rolling back to keep her with him, both arms still wrapped round her, lean hands smoothing over her slender back with warm affection.

'I'm crazy about you, too,' Lara whispered, sinking deeper into contentment, a drowsy smile on her lips as she rested her head down on his shoulder, her nostrils flaring at the achingly familiar scent of his skin. She had the loving, supportive family that she had always craved and in addition she had Gaetano and their children. Life was better than she had ever believed it could be.

* * * * *

If you thought The King's Christmas Heir *was magical then you're sure to fall in love with the first and second instalments in* The Stefanos Legacy *trilogy*

Promoted to the Greek's Wife
The Heirs His Housekeeper Carried
Both available now!

Also, why not dive into these other Lynne Graham stories?

Christmas Babies for the Italian
The Greek's Convenient Cinderella
The Ring the Spaniard Gave Her
Cinderella's Desert Baby Bombshell
Her Best Royal Kept Secret

Available now!